THE SCANDALOUS LADY SANDFORD

ADELE CLEE

This is a work of fiction. All names, characters, places and incidents are products of the author's imagination. All characters are fictitious and any resemblance to real persons, living or dead, is purely coincidental.

No part of this book may be copied or reproduced in any manner without the author's permission.

Cover designed by **Jay Aheer**

Books by Adele Clee

To Save a Sinner

A Curse of the Heart

What Every Lord Wants

The Secret To Your Surrender

A Simple Case of Seduction

Anything for Love Series

What You Desire

What You Propose

What You Deserve

What You Promised

The Brotherhood Series

Lost to the Night

Slave to the Night

Abandoned to the Night

Lured to the Night

Lost Ladies of London

The Mysterious Miss Flint

The Deceptive Lady Darby

The Scandalous Lady Sandford

The Daring Miss Darcy

CHAPTER ONE

R ows of red lanterns hung from the trees in the Grove at Vauxhall Pleasure Gardens. The clang of cymbals drew everyone's gaze to the Prussian military band settling into their seats in the bandstand. Those already merry on punch tutted and moaned for they preferred the light-hearted country dancing to the solemn sound of a soldier's drum.

Lady Lillian Sandford jumped upon hearing the high-pitched call of the bugle. "They should give us a warning before blasting out a tune."

Her brother, Ross Sandford, Marquess of Trevane, snorted in amusement. "A bugle call *is* a warning. It's supposed to get the crowd's attention."

The loud bang of drums sent Lillian's nerves scattering. Though of late, it did not take much to unsettle her equilibrium. The image of the black coach flashed into her mind. For three consecutive nights, she'd witnessed the conveyance crawl around Berkeley Square before stopping beneath the lamp outside her window. Perhaps the coachman meant to frighten her with his pockmarked face and toothless grin. Perhaps his beady stare was an ominous warning. But for what?

She'd seen the same coach this evening, parked on Mount Street.

By rights, she should mention it to Vane, but her brother's need to protect her proved stifling. Guilt formed the basis of his obsessive nature. He'd been her shadow for the last two years. No one dared speak of her shame in his presence. No one looked her way for fear of encountering Vane's wrath. He'd shot the rogue who ruined her and would pull a pistol on any man who attempted to do so again.

As the music grew in pitch and tempo, Lillian clutched Vane's arm.

He cast her a sidelong glance. "What is it? You're shivering. Has someone spoken out of turn?" Straightening to his full height, he scoured the crowd, his eyes ablaze and ready to rain bolts of fire on anyone who so much as looked in their direction.

"Of course not." No one conversed with her. "To these people, I'm invisible." The tightness in her chest made it hard to breathe, and she touched the gold locket at her throat for it always brought comfort. "I'm the only lady who hasn't danced."

Respectable gentlemen considered her a leper. Rakes and scoundrels treated her as they would a nun—a woman strictly out of bounds, not one of superior status. And so she lingered within an empty void, unworthy in every regard.

"Why would you want to court attention from these degenerates?" Vane gestured to the two fools standing to their left, laughing as they marched to the band's rhythmical beat.

"I do not want attention, Vane, but it would be nice for someone to acknowledge I exist." Was a nod or a genuine smile from a gentleman too much to ask? "Is it wrong to crave companionship? Perhaps then I might not feel so alone."

Vane frowned. "You're not alone. You have me."

How could she tell him she was suffocating under the weight of his protection? How could she hurt him when he'd given up everything to keep her safe? "After all that occurred with Lord Martin—"

"Do not dare utter that rogue's name in my presence." A dark expression marred Vane's handsome countenance. "Tell me what to do. Tell me how to make things right."

"You could talk to me. Something is troubling you. After months of hiding indoors, we've spent the last week traipsing up and down every street in London, and yet you refuse to tell me why."

Vane turned his head so she had no hope of reading his reaction.

"And why insist on coming to Vauxhall?" she continued, determined to have an answer. "There are hundreds of people here tonight. Must you torture me like this?"

That got his attention. He swung around, his blue eyes hard and unyielding. "Torture you? I've not slept in days."

The admission brought a wave of relief. At least Vane's odd mood was not a figment of her imagination.

Lillian touched his arm. "You can be honest with me, Vane. If you're tired of living in the shadows, if—"

"It's not that," he snapped.

The band played their last note, and the crowd applauded with mild enthusiasm. At the sound of the supper whistle, the excitement in the Grove reached fever pitch as people scrambled to find their assigned table.

"Come." Vane led her away from the bandstand to the open supper boxes located along the colonnade, and she knew that was the end of their conversation. "We're in box nine. Let's try to enjoy the evening."

While no one gave Lillian a passing glance, Vane never failed to attract attention. Ladies brushed past him on purpose and gripped his arm to steady their balance. They batted their lashes, drooled and sighed, slipped notes into his coat pocket. And yet he ignored every comment, ignored every written request to sneak away to a secluded part of the garden and partake in a little wild sport.

A weary sigh left Vane's lips as they settled into their seats. Lord Martin had stolen more than Lillian's virtue. He'd stolen her brother's happiness, too.

"Why not escort me home and then return to Vauxhall? Did I not see Lord Ashbourne near the rotunda?" Lillian examined the platter of cold meat and salad placed before her. "You were friends once I seem to recall."

Vane swallowed a mouthful of wine. "We were inseparable." He meant in his carefree days before the scandal. "Now we move in different circles."

Guilt flared. She was to blame for their estrangement. Naivety was a trait of the damned it seemed.

"Besides," Vane continued, "I know you're excited about seeing Mr Green's coal gas balloon."

Lillian smiled. "They say his balloon takes passengers." She often envisioned climbing into the basket and drifting off to a faraway land where no one judged her—where she would be free to do as she pleased.

"Only a fool would risk his neck in such a flimsy contraption."

"I wonder what it's like drifting so close to the stars?"

Vane glanced to the heavens. "Cold, damp and frightfully boring."

"You used to be game for anything." Lillian sipped her fruit punch though it tasted tart rather than sweet.

"When a gentleman has responsibilities, he cannot afford to gamble with his life."

Lillian's heart sank. Through her own stupidity, she'd become an iron chain around her brother's neck. "With any luck, a gentleman will come along to relieve you of your burden."

"You're not a burden, Lillian. And perhaps you're right. One day you may find someone who makes you happy." Vane smiled, though something in his tone suggested she would be a fool to hope.

Was this to be her life now? Hiding in the shadows, never knowing friendship or true love.

They fell into a companionable silence while they finished their supper although her brother studied every person who happened to walk by.

Vane emptied the contents of the carafe into his glass and drank it down. "We need to make our way along the central avenue if we want to watch the balloon. I suggest we leave now before there's a stampede."

They had no fear of being crushed. Everyone gave them a wide berth. No one dared to smack shoulders with a man like Vane.

As Lillian edged out from the table, she lost her footing and almost stumbled. Vane caught her by the elbow. "Are you all right?"

A chuckle escaped her lips. "It's the fruit punch. I don't know what they've put in it, but the concoction is rather potent."

Vane turned back to the table and examined the empty glass. "And yet you drank every drop."

Lillian shrugged. "Ignore me. No doubt I stood too quickly." She placed her hand in the crook of Vane's arm. Her head felt light and woozy, but she did not want to worry him. "Come, a stroll will soon set me right."

"A stroll? We may have to sprint if we want to beat the crowd."

Vane led her out through the Grove and along the gravel walkway. Everyone else seemed just as eager to reach the large crimson balloon swaying gently in the distance. Groups of people poured out through the gaps between the trees, most of them loud and boisterous after downing copious amounts of wine at supper.

"Mr Green takes questions and explains the science behind ballooning," Vane said. "It has something to do with gas being lighter than atmospheric air."

Vane told her about numerous disasters, of people falling to their death, of lightning strikes and sparks from fireworks sending one balloon up in flames. Suddenly, the thought of flying to destinations new seemed unappealing.

"Is that why they wait for thirty minutes until after the balloon has ascended before lighting the fireworks?"

"Undoubtedly."

They joined the assembled throng gathered around the wooden platform supporting the eighty-foot balloon. Made of crimson silk and covered with netting, it took six men tugging on ropes to anchor it down. The light summer breeze had gathered momentum, and the approaching clumps of black cloud did not bode well for a trouble-free ascent. No doubt alarmed by the sudden change in the weather, Mr Green clambered inside the basket along with another gentleman who bellowed orders to those gripping the ropes.

"It appears Mr Green is in a hurry tonight." Lillian watched the flurry of activity. Perhaps whatever gas kept the contraption in the air was affecting her, too, as lights danced before her eyes and it became difficult to focus.

Vane glanced up at the menacing cloud. "Green had better take off soon else he'll get caught in the storm." Raising a brow of disapproval, he perused her gown. "Did I not tell you to bring your cloak this evening?"

While the cut of her lavender dress was conservative by most ladies' standards, the fine material did little to keep the cold at bay. "But it was so mild when we left." Was it her imagination or did her words sound slurred?

"Release the ropes!" Mr Green cried. "Steady, now. Steady as she goes." He tried to smile as he doffed his hat and waved to the excited onlookers. No sooner had the basket begun its slow ascent from the platform than a gust of wind whipped underneath. One man lost his grip on the rope, and the whole contraption lurched forward.

The crowd gasped and edged back. Some people covered their heads with their hands. Others cowered behind the person standing next to them.

"There's nothing to fear." Mr Green's cries of reassurance failed to calm the nervous bystanders.

"For heaven's sake," Vane muttered. "Hysterics only make matters worse. Green is a capable man. He knows how to deal with these unforeseen eventualities."

Another man released his rope too quickly. Mr Green continued to shout instructions as the balloon swayed back and forth, groaning and creaking as it strained against its moorings.

Panic forced people to turn and run. No one gave a hoot that Lillian was a social leper. Nor did they fear a punch on the nose from Vane. Amidst the pandemonium, drunken revellers pushed and barged past them. Lillian made the mistake of letting go of Vane's arm and was carried away by a surge of people charging towards the entrance.

Chaos erupted despite Mr Green's ability to control his giant bag of air.

Jostled between two gentlemen, Lillian struggled to keep sight of Vane. It didn't help that the sea of heads blurred into one colourful wave. She grew dizzier by the minute. Confused. Bewildered. Events seemed to happen around her as though she sat in the supper booth, a mere spectator.

One muscular arm clamped around her waist and dragged her back against a hard, solid chest. The sickly sweet scent of rum flooded her nostrils, coupled with the briny smell of the sea. Sleep beckoned. The world swirled. Her head lolled forward, the heavy weight of her eyelids dragging her down into the darkness.

Events appeared in fractured pictures. She recalled being carried through the trees, noted the crimson balloon drifting across the sky, growing smaller and smaller as she lay on her back in a rowboat. Spots of rain landed on her cheek, but she lacked the strength to move. She thought to cry out, but despite her terrible experiences with Lord Martin, she wasn't scared.

"Give her a drink, Mackenzie," one oarsman said as he used brute strength to propel the vessel along the Thames. "A few drops of laudanum will see her right till we reach the ship."

The ship?

The hulking man beside her pulled a brown bottle from his pocket and removed the stopper. "Here, lass, a quick sip will make for a more pleasant journey." With one hand supporting her head, the Scot pressed the bottle to her lips. "There's nothing to fear." His tone was calm, soothing, yet he gave her no option but to drink. "The master needs your help that's all."

An image of Vane, frantically scouring the crowd, flashed into her head. "Wh-where's my brother?"

"Don't worry about your brother, lass. No doubt you'll see him soon enough." He lowered her head back down onto the sack, slipped the bottle into his pocket and then shrugged out of his greatcoat and placed it over her like a blanket. "Rest is all you need now."

Lillian's lids grew heavy, but the loud cracks and bangs overhead forced her to look up as the fireworks erupted. Streams of red and gold lights sparkled like jewels in the night sky. She continued watching the display until her eyes were dead weights and she drifted into a peaceful slumber.

Lillian woke to the sound of lapping water and creaking wood. She touched her temple to ease the dull ache and then sat up and surveyed her surroundings. Daylight streamed through the large windows spanning the width of the great cabin: the captain's quarters. Maps and nautical instruments littered the huge oak table. The man was an adventurer, one who embraced risk. Red velvet curtains separated the small poster bed from the room that held books, a music stand, bow and fiddle ... the tools of an educated man. She suppressed a chuckle when her gaze fell to the range of swords filling an open chest. Despite the captain's obvious intelligence, he'd made a grave error. He doubted a woman's ability to wield a sword.

A key rattled in the lock, and she curled into a ball on the bed and feigned sleep. At the heavy trudge of footsteps on the boards, she peered through half-closed eyes and watched the man they called Mackenzie place a pewter plate and a flagon on the table.

She contemplated charging at him, thumping his chest and demanding to know what he was about, but she lacked the strength of mind and body.

Mackenzie turned and looked at her, strode over and touched her lightly on the arm. "I've brought food for you, lass."

Lillian blinked, yawned and stretched one arm above her head. "What time is it?"

"Almost noon," Mackenzie said in a soft Scottish burr. "With a good wind in the sails, we'll reach our destination come nightfall."

"Are we away to France?"

"Lord, no. We're sailing along the South Coast. We'll drop anchor for a couple of hours while we take on ... cargo, then we'll be on our way." Mackenzie drew his hand down his beard. "Rest here now. I'll lock the door for your own safety. The master will be none too pleased if you tumble overboard."

"Will your master—"

9

"Now is not the time for questions. I'll return when it's safe to come up on deck."

The Scot left the room. The heavy clunk of a key confirmed he'd locked the door.

Lillian spent an hour looking through the books on the shelf while she ate. Her captor read Latin, studied Socrates and Plato. From the music sheets, he had a fondness for Haydn. After a poor attempt at striking a tune on the fiddle, she settled back on the bed and let sleep take her.

Hours passed. She woke to a room bathed in moonlight.

Grabbing the burgundy coverlet from the bed, she draped it over her shoulders and padded to the door. She pressed her ear to the thin gap between the frame and the jamb but heard nothing in the corridor beyond. The glint of a brass key in the lock caught her eye. Mackenzie must have returned. She turned it and eased open the door, relieved to find there were no guards keeping watch.

Lillian crept along the narrow corridor and up a flight of steps leading to the deck. The chill in the air stole her breath, as did the giant moon casting an eerie silver-green sheen over the sea. The wind whipped strands of hair loose from her dishevelled coiffure and, despite her dire circumstances, for a moment she felt free.

The men going about their work paid her no heed, and so she wandered over to the wooden rail and peered at the inky depths below.

Did they imagine she lacked the courage to jump?

"The water is icy cold tonight, lass." The Scot's deep voice startled her. "Stiff muscles are a hindrance when it comes to swimming. You'd be lucky to last thirty seconds in there."

Lillian did not turn to acknowledge him but stared out at the horizon. He came to stand beside her. Neither of them spoke. His heavy breathing left puffs of white mist in the chilly night air. Soon the silence became deafening.

"Were you with the man who stopped the carriage outside my window?"

"Aye."

Lillian cast him a sidelong glance and studied his face. With soft blue eyes, full cheeks and a red beard tinged with white flecks, the Scot's countenance suggested his heart was as large as his frame.

"Am I here because of my brother?" It wouldn't be the first time a man had used her to exact his revenge.

"Aye. It's not for me to explain the details, but know you're in no danger, lass. We'll not harm a hair on your head. Master's orders."

Truth echoed in his words. Indeed, she should have been terrified out of her wits, and yet she felt a strange form of peace.

"Who is your master?" She looked the Scot in the eye. "Do I know him?"

The Scot's mouth twitched into the beginnings of a smile. "Happen you do. I have it on good authority he's a friend."

Lillian had no friends.

"Aren't friends supposed to extend an invitation when they seek your company?"

He opened his mouth to answer, but a loud cry from the crow's nest drew their attention to the black mass of land in the distance.

"Not long to wait now." The Scot inclined his head. "Should you need anything during your stay at the castle, just ask for Mackenzie." He patted his chest so there was no mistaking who he meant.

The castle? This whole debacle was like something one read about in the gothic novels of Ann Radcliffe and the like. "Thank you, Mackenzie. I only hope your master shows me the same care and consideration you have."

"Have no doubt. The master is a gentleman despite what others might say. Now, I'd best attend to my duties."

Mackenzie strode away.

Wrapping the coverlet tightly around her shoulders, Lillian stood and watched as they drew closer to the shore. Mackenzie returned, thrust a telescope into her hand and left without saying a word. It was difficult to see in the dark, but she spotted the tall brazier emitting an amber glow from the top of the castle's keep.

Someone shouted about dropping a temporary anchor, and she soon found herself bundled into a small boat. Mackenzie and another man rowed to the sandy cove. They led her up the steep stone path to the castle on the clifftop, escorted her through the gatehouse and the bailey, before coming to an abrupt halt outside studded oak doors.

"The master is waiting for you in the great hall." Mackenzie offered her a reassuring grin. "You're on your own from here."

She handed Mackenzie the coverlet. She'd sooner catch her death of cold than appear as a frail woman swamped in a blanket. Both men bowed and left her standing in the damp corridor.

Lillian inhaled deeply and squared her shoulders, ready to meet the only man brave enough to challenge Vane.

CHAPTER TWO

F abian Darcy lounged back in the majestic throne chair positioned in the middle of the dais. Some of his men were out scouring the streets of London and Paris looking for his sister, Estelle. Another group had the task of finding the Marquess of Trevane's sister and bringing her to Raven Island.

The creak of the centuries-old door drew his attention. His heart hadn't stopped pounding since Graves woke him to say he'd spotted a ship approaching. Fabian had stood by the brazier on the roof of the keep and watched the small boat ferry his guest ashore. He imagined Vane's distress upon discovering he'd failed to protect the only person who mattered.

It was a feeling Fabian knew well.

The soft pad of footsteps on the stone floor forced him to focus. Lady Lillian Sandford walked towards him with the same regal air she'd possessed as a child. A satisfied grin threatened to form, but he dismissed it along with the secret fascination he'd nurtured since boyhood.

"Lady Lillian." He jumped to his feet, delighting in the look of instant recognition, and relief flashing in her eyes. Her hair was as dark as he remembered, her lips as pink and full. "Welcome to my humble abode."

A frown marred her pretty brow. She searched his face before scanning his unconventional attire. No doubt she preferred seeing a gentleman in a starched cravat and tight-fitting coat, not an open-collared shirt hanging over buckskin breeches.

"Lord Ravenscroft." The lady curtsied. "Or should I call you the Raven? That is the name you use when sailing the high seas, is it not?"

So, she had kept abreast of his movements in recent years. "Merchants must have faith that their goods will reach the destination without incident. The name merely conveys confidence that I'm a man who gets the job done."

"Oh, I wondered if it was a reference to your obsidian eyes and ebony locks, although my brother is more inclined to believe it has something to do with your black heart."

Fabian gritted his teeth. The mere mention of Vane caused him to clench his fists at his sides. For eight years he'd dreamed of knocking the rogue on his arse and taking aim. But firing a ball into Vane's chest would not bring Estelle back. And if Fabian's current plan had any hope of success, he had to remain calm and composed.

"The raven is a symbol of good luck, or so I'd have my clients believe. Equally, they are opportunistic birds. They take what they can where they can find it." And that's exactly how he'd made his fortune, taking the jobs others deemed too risky.

The lady narrowed her gaze. "When it comes to kidnapping, I have to agree that both luck and opportunity played a part. How fortunate that Mr Green had a mishap with his balloon."

Knowing his men, it was no mishap but the result of meticulous skill and planning. "While I'm yet to hear the details of their mission, my men know to take advantage of any situation." He cast her a mischievous grin. "As do I, Lillian."

Damn. He hadn't meant to use her given name, or for his voice to carry a sensual undertone. Still, from what he'd heard, she was accustomed to gentlemen being far too familiar. The thought roused his ire.

"Then they must get their thieving ability from their master." She touched the gold locket resting at the base of her throat as though it had a magical ability to bring the wearer courage. "Are you not a pirate, my lord? Are you not a man used to taking what he wants?"

Fabian laughed. "Is that what your brother told you? Perhaps the thought that he's not the only scoundrel helps him sleep easier at night."

"So you deny the allegation?"

"I run a legitimate business, but believe what you will." He stepped down from the dais, and the lady stepped back. "Stealing you away from home is the only criminal act I've ever committed, and so on that count, I raise my hands guilty as charged."

"One thing is certain," she said, lifting her chin.

"And what is that?"

"I'm looking at a dead man. My brother will kill you and leave your head on a spike as a warning to those who dare to cross him."

Fabian folded his arms across his chest. "Would you care to make a wager to that effect?"

"I know him better than anyone. It won't matter that we were once friends and neighbours. You'd be a fool to underestimate him." A weary sigh left her lips. "After all, what has he to lose?"

"What have any of us to lose?" He closed the gap between them. "Vane robbed me of the only thing that mattered. Perhaps it's time I returned the favour." Oh, it was a fitting retribution: an eye for an eye, a sister for a sister.

"You speak as though I should fear you, my lord." She bit down on her bottom lip as she watched his every move. She looked pale and tired though not from lack of sleep. "And yet I must admit to being relieved to find you're my captor."

"Then allow me to advise you to have a care. I'm no longer the sweet young man you remember." Hate and bitterness filled his heart now, and he made sure she heard it in his voice. Her family's evil actions had purged him of any romantic notions he might have once possessed. "Don't make the mistake of trusting me. Don't imagine for a minute that I won't use you to get what I want."

"And what *do* you want, Fabian?" She shuffled back a few steps and surveyed the vaulted ceiling, the fan of swords on the wall above the dais, and the vast array of antlers displayed as trophies from successful hunts. "Why act the wicked baron and bring me to a castle in the middle of Lord knows where? Had you asked for my help or guidance, I would have given it freely."

The sound of his given name falling from her lips threw him off kilter although only momentarily. "It is not *your* help I need."

She stared at him for a moment and swallowed deeply. "I see." Those two words held a wealth of pain and disappointment. "You mean to use me in the hope my brother will fall at your feet and do whatever you ask. Am I to be played and discarded like a pawn in your bid to capture the king?"

Guilt surfaced and to cleanse his conscience he thought of Estelle, suffering in squalor for eight years while the world presumed her dead.

"Estelle is alive." He squeezed the words past the lump in his throat.

A stunned silence filled the vast hall.

"Alive?" Lillian's eyes grew wide. She jerked her head back and clutched her locket. "But she perished when *The Torrens* sank off the French coast."

Fabian's heart thumped in his chest as he pictured his sweet sister struggling to stay afloat amid a sea of bloated bodies and the remains of the wooden wreckage. "I have every reason to believe she survived."

"But how can that be?" Lillian shook her head, confusion swimming in her hazel eyes. The lack of light in the gloomy hall made her irises appear earthy brown, yet he knew they were ringed with a hypnotic shade of green. Indeed, he daren't look too closely for fear of falling under their spell. "Why has she not come home?"

"How can she? She doesn't know where home is." Besides his men, few knew the island's location. "When Estelle ran away my father owned Prescott Hall. We lost everything when we invested in your father's mining venture."

A cold chill swept over him. He would never forget the pained look on his father's face when he delivered the devastating news. They'd had no choice but to break the entail as Fabian would have struggled to maintain the property under the burden of such a heavy debt.

A blush touched Lillian's cheeks. "My father was a frivolous man who cared nothing for other men's hardships."

The hint of shame in her voice pleased him. "In that, we agree."

"Then am I to understand that this impressive building is a recent purchase?"

"My first ship was my home for several years. Now I have the funds to live wherever I please."

It suited him to live away from the society he despised. Gentlemen were fickle. A lord could rob a man of his wealth and blame it on a bad investment. When a poor man took advantage of the rich, they called him a thief and a pirate.

"And it pleases you to hide away here?"

Fabian straightened. Lillian Sandford had always known what to say to rile him. "What are you insinuating? You may call me a pirate, but do not label me a coward." He'd beaten men to a pulp for less. "I live here because I cannot bear hypocrisy. I live here because I can do what I damn well please whenever I choose."

"How fortunate." Her hazel eyes searched his face, probing, accessing. "Like all birds, the raven is a symbol of freedom. As a woman, doing what I please is a luxury I can ill afford."

The comment brought about an unexpected tightening in his chest. "Walk with me." It was a command, not a request. He could no longer stand there looking into those sorrowful pools and pretend to feel nothing.

They left the great hall and climbed the stairs to the top of the keep. Neither spoke though guilt flared when he heard her breathless pants but did not offer his assistance.

He led her to the brazier. The dying flames gave off enough heat to keep the chill in the air at bay. "Look out and tell me what you see."

Sailors stared at the wide stretch of ocean, their minds engaged in planning their next wild adventure. Lillian gazed up at the full moon, at the stars twinkling in the inky sky. The vastness often made a person feel insignificant. For others, the majesty of it all proved powerful enough to cleanse the soul. Her little sighs and gasps told him she took comfort from the peace and stillness of the night.

"It is hard to comprehend how something so magnificent can exist in such a cruel world," she said softly. Did she speak of a past suffering, or of her distress upon being kidnapped by a pirate?

"Nature causes just as much devastation as man. Ask anyone who's sailed during a thunderstorm or been swamped by thirty-foot waves." He thought of Estelle scrambling to keep her head above the water and quickly sought a way to change the subject. "Hold out your arms and twirl around, but keep your fingers wide apart."

She turned and frowned at his odd request. "Why?" Perhaps she thought he meant to ridicule her.

"Do it, and then I shall tell you."

"What, so you may mock me?" She ventured closer to the parapet and peered at the jagged rocks below. "Or is it your intention to make me dizzy? Would it suit your plan if I tumbled over the edge and plunged to my death?"

Panic gripped him. Fabian closed the gap between them. Surely the woman wasn't fool enough to jump. "I've spent eight years blaming myself for Estelle's death." Vane was culpable, too. "I'll not have yours on my conscience."

"And yet you kidnapped me and brought me here to live with a crew of seafaring men." She stepped back, an incredulous look distorting her pretty features. "Do you think the matrons will accept me now? In our society, a woman with a ruined reputation may as well be dead."

"From what I hear it is too late to worry about your virtue." He hadn't meant his words to sound so blunt, but anger burned inside. It was too late to offer advice about the company she kept, and he blamed Vane for her lack of judgement. "Only marriage can save you now."

"Marriage?" Lillian gave a mocking snort. "How foolish of me. Why did I not think of it before? I'll simply pick one of the many men clambering over each other to marry the disreputable sister of a scoundrel."

Fabian fell silent. He relished those few seconds of peace, for his world was about to erupt into a cacophony of questions and protests. "Why pick another man when you can marry me?"

CHAPTER THREE

"Marry you! Are you out of your mind?" Lillian swallowed to clear the lump in her throat. This was not the first time Fabian Darcy had tormented her for his own amusement. "Is that your penance for kidnapping? Or is this where you lie and tell me you've admired me since I was a girl?"

"That depends. Does my motive have any bearing on your answer?"

The breeze caught the open neck of his shirt, drawing her gaze to the bronzed skin beneath. She'd spied on him once, had seen his bare chest as he wrestled with Vane on the lawn one summer's evening when her parents were away. His shoulders were broader now. Judging by the muscular thighs filling his breeches, she imagined the rest of him was equally impressive.

"You need a husband," he continued, "and I seem to be the only man offering."

"Have you offered? It sounded more like a cruel joke to me." Before she could utter another word, Fabian grabbed her hand. The sudden jolt of awareness made her gasp. "Let go of me." She tried to break free, but his grip was firm.

"Will you do me the honour of becoming my wife?" He brought her hand to his mouth and brushed his warm lips over her knuckles. Every nerve in her body sprang to life. He gazed deeply into her eyes, and for a moment he looked sincere. "Marry me, Lillian."

"Don't be ridiculous." Lillian shook her head as he released her hand. Her stomach flipped, and she felt giddy. Perhaps she was still suffering from the effects of the punch. "Is it to be retribution, then? Are you so intent on punishing Vane that you would shackle yourself to me?"

Fabian shrugged one shoulder. "I must admit, the thought of causing your brother pain pleases me no end."

A small part of her wished he had lied. Could he not have said he found her enchanting? Could he not have invented a fairy tale? One that spoke of a destitute lord making his fortune on the high seas so he could return to claim a lost love.

But this had nothing to do with love. This was a clear act of spite and revenge.

"What makes you think I'm desperate enough to accept?" It didn't matter that she'd dreamt of marrying him when she was fifteen and he was a happy, carefree gentleman of twenty. "You may despise my brother, but I love him. What makes you think I would hurt him by frolicking with his enemy?"

The corners of Fabian's mouth curled up into a sinful smile. "Are you not a woman who craves adventure? Does the thought of frolicking with a pirate not hold some fascination?"

"Not anymore." Once, she'd told him she planned to see the world, to dance beneath the stars in exotic locations. The two years spent in Italy were equivalent to a lifetime in Hell. Now all she wanted was someone to talk to, someone who cared and might one day grow to love her.

Fabian searched her face. "You've always put Vane first. Is it not time to consider your needs? Is he not the reason you're in this predicament? And I speak of your ruined reputation, not the fact I rescued you from a tedious existence."

A weak chuckle escaped her lips, although he was right in one respect. Life was exceedingly dull. "I've never been selfish. What I want, you cannot give me." She wanted love, devotion and trust but the Raven's tainted heart lacked the capacity for anything other than vengeance.

"That's where you're wrong." He closed the gap between them, reached into her coiffure, pulled out the pins and discarded them on the floor. "I know exactly what you want."

"What are you doing?" Her knees almost buckled as the pads of his fingers tangled in her hair. She should have slapped his hand away but the intimacy of the moment fed the starving loneliness within.

"Here, you can do as you please." He caressed one ebony curl as it slipped through his fingers. "There is no one to judge you. Wear your hair down, let the wind blow every strand free. Dress in breeches if you so desire."

He stood too close. The unique scent of his skin teased her nostrils, a combination of leather, spice and the salty sea air. Dark stubble covered his sculpted jaw. The sound of his voice proved hypnotic.

What was it he promised if not love?

"Here, you need not wear silk." His fingers skimmed the sleeves of her gown, and she shivered when they drifted towards the base of her throat and settled on her gold locket. "You have no need for trinkets or baubles." He wrapped his fingers around the chain, and for one heart-stopping moment, she thought he was about to rip it from her neck.

Fear gripped her, crushing the last breath from her lungs. "Get your damn hands off my locket." The words came out exactly as she intended: a low, menacing growl.

Fabian jerked his head back and pulled his hand away as if he'd touched metal fresh from the furnace.

"You may do what the hell you want to me." To some extent, she'd given up caring. "But touch that locket again, and you'll be begging for Vane to come and save you." Bile burned in her throat when she thought of losing her prized possession. "Do not test me, Fabian, else you may discover that I am no longer the sweet young girl you remember."

Sucking in a deep breath, he inclined his head by way of an apology. "What is so precious—"

"And don't ask me about it," she interjected, "not ever." Only one person knew what she kept close to her heart, and he would never betray her.

The muscle in Fabian's cheek flexed, but he said nothing. An uncomfortable silence ensued, the deafening sound only broken by the crashing of waves on the rocks below.

"I can offer you the one thing you desire above all else." Fabian spoke softly, all arrogance abandoned. "I offer you freedom."

For a lady, the power to make decisions was a treasure beyond that of gold and jewels. But she'd had naivety knocked out of her by a cold-hearted devil. She knew the words men used to manipulate situations to their advantage.

"You cannot offer marriage and freedom. It is a contradiction in terms. Marriage is a means for a man to exert his control. A wife must do her husband's bidding."

"Not if you married me."

"I would be your property, a commodity to exploit in any manner you saw fit."

"I demand nothing from you." He gestured to the vast landscape stretching beyond the castle walls. "I offer you an island, a place to live and roam freely. I can have a house built if you'd rather not live with me in the castle."

To live away from society proved tempting. Fabian made no promises. All he wanted was a means to control her brother. "But to gain my freedom, I must betray Vane."

Fabian pushed his hand through his hair. "It is not betrayal if Vane doesn't give a damn about me. Had he bothered to reply to my missive, we would not be standing here. I am the one who bears a grudge, and rightly so."

"What happened to Estelle was not Vane's fault." Vane would have disobeyed their father and married Estelle if only she'd given him a chance.

"Damn right it was." Vehemence brimmed in his voice. "Vane could have saved her, but he let pride and arrogance get in the way."

"And how will marrying me help you now? Do you think revenge brings peace? Because let me tell you it does not." She stared at him, and he struggled to hold her gaze. "Tell me the truth, Fabian. You owe me that at least."

He gave a curt nod of resignation. "Come, let me show you to your room. It's growing chilly, and the hour is late. I'll explain everything on the way."

The stairs seemed steeper on the descent. Twice she almost slipped on the worn stone steps. Fabian reached up and captured her hand. The sudden jolt of awareness only unbalanced her further. As he firmed his grip, she could feel the callouses on his palm. The Raven didn't sit on a throne and bark orders. She imagined him working alongside his men, standing at the helm of his ship during long, perilous voyages, risking his life to restore the family fortune.

They reached the door to the landing, and he released her hand. "We do business with merchants in Paris," he suddenly said. "Recently, one of my most trusted men journeyed to the city to deliver important documents."

Did he speak of Mackenzie? There was something in the

Scot's voice that instilled confidence, something solid and dependable.

Fabian gestured to the long corridor, candles in iron sconces lighting their way. He clasped his hands behind his back as they fell into a slow pace. "Mackenzie has seen the miniature I have of Estelle. While leaving the merchant's house in a hurry, he bumped into a woman and knocked her books out of her hand. He stopped to help her, but it was only as he watched her scurry away that he noted the likeness."

Lillian's heart sank. Oh, she wanted to believe Estelle was alive, not just for Fabian's sake. Vane had not been the same since the day Estelle ran away from Prescott Hall. He nurtured a darkness deep within, a hardened heart and an utter lack of sentiment for the fair sex.

"When one longs to reunite with a loved one, the mind can play many tricks," she said. The painful lump in her throat was a precursor to the well of tears filling her eyes. She glanced away quickly. "When we are desperate, we will believe anything."

He remained silent for a moment, and she could feel the heat of his gaze drifting over her. "I've spent the last eight years staring at women with black hair and mesmerising eyes, hoping they were someone else."

"I imagine you see Estelle wherever you go." She found the strength to look at him.

"Indeed, although it is not only the dead who haunt our dreams." He stared into her eyes and then blinked and shook his head. "Despite doubting Mackenzie, we returned together to Paris, took the miniature and knocked on doors in the quarter, asked at circulating libraries, at cafes, walked the promenades."

"Is the miniature a good likeness?"

"You may judge for yourself." Fabian strode to a door further along the corridor and had to duck slightly to clear the stone lintel.

Lillian waited outside. A lady did not enter a gentleman's bedchamber. And yet she wanted to see where Fabian slept, what trinkets lay on his side table, what the intimate surroundings said about the man.

Fabian returned and handed Lillian the oval miniature. "It is all I have of hers."

The artist had captured Estelle's likeness perfectly. She had a face one instantly fell in love with. It had nothing to do with her classical beauty: porcelain skin, full pink lips and wide dark eyes. When one looked at Estelle, they saw kindness, sincerity, a generosity of spirit.

Lillian traced the outline of the picture with her finger. "You must miss her terribly. You were always close."

"Not a day goes by that I don't think of her."

"I understand." Oh, she understood in a way he could not comprehend. "I take it you had no luck finding her in Paris."

"On the contrary, we discovered she was working as a governess for a wealthy merchant. The man's wife recognised her instantly and confirmed that Estelle had lived with them for a year. But she packed her things and left the day Mackenzie encountered her in the street. I have reason to believe she boarded a ship to England, but the trail ends there."

Lillian could hear the frustration in his voice, the anxiety that came from fear and uncertainty. "And you want Vane's help to find her?"

Fabian took the miniature and glanced at the image of his sister. "Vane spent time with Estelle before she left Prescott Hall. I must know what they discussed. What happened between them to make her run away? In London, men fear your brother. No man is more equipped to find Estelle."

Everything Fabian said made perfect sense. Vane commanded attention wherever he went. He had friends in high places, an equal amount of lowlife acquaintances occupying the backstreet dens and rookeries.

"And yet you say you've contacted him and he has refused to offer his assistance." Of late, Vane appeared morose and withdrawn. He was drinking too much, struggled to sleep. Did the change in him stem from the sighting of Estelle?

"As requested, Vane sent his reply to the Eight Bells in Wapping. He refuses to believe my sister is alive and insists I leave him the hell alone."

"I see." Vane did not want to dwell on painful memories of the past. Who could blame him? "And so instead you sent the pock-faced man to scare me out of my wits. You spirited me away from home and brought me here to force my brother's hand."

Fabian frowned. "My men were under strict instructions to ensure no harm came to you. If they've—"

"They drugged me, Fabian." The fruit punch contained some sort of sleep-inducing medicine so she would be more compliant. "You have harmed me in more ways than I can count. Heaven knows who saw them carry me to the rowboat. Because of your idiotic plan I cannot go home."

Frustration made her heart race. What was she to do now? She clenched her fists and contemplated punching him hard in the chest. As if she'd not dealt with enough these last two years, God sought to punish her further.

"The solution to your problem is evident." Fabian's tone carried a hint of arrogance. "Marry me and live here."

Damn him. If she were a man, they'd settle this dispute with pistols. "And that is what you offer for the trouble you've caused?"

"It is a damn sight more than Vane offered Estelle."

Unable to control the sudden burst of anger, she lashed out, but Fabian caught her by the wrist.

"I know you so well I can predict your every move." A

mischievous glint flashed in his coal-black eyes. He held her so close she could feel the heat radiating from his body. "I know you chew the inside of your cheek when you're nervous. I know the hitch in your voice when you're lying."

"You know the girl, not the woman." Lillian's breath came too quickly. Tragic events had changed her, and she would never be that carefree girl again. "I'm not the same person you remember."

Fabian's gaze drifted over her face. "I think you are."

Lillian almost chuckled. How could he claim to know her when she no longer recognised herself? "I'm tainted, ruined, a poor example to womankind."

A growl rumbled in the back of his throat. "And I blame Vane for his lack of guidance."

Oh, they were going around in circles. "You cannot blame Vane for everything." Lillian pulled her arm free from Fabian's grasp and stepped away. "Show me to my room. I'm tired. My head hurts, and I cannot think anymore."

"As you wish." Fabian gestured to the door situated a little further along the corridor. "You're in the room next to mine. Come." He strode past her, opened the door and disappeared inside.

With some hesitance, she followed him. Upon entering, her gaze moved to the four-poster bed with gold curtains, to the low beam ceiling and the wrought iron chandelier. Someone had been in to light the fire in the stone hearth and to turn down the plush coverlet on the bed.

The medieval-inspired room made Lillian feel as though she'd stepped back in time. This enchanting castle was so far removed from the ugly world she knew. One could lose themselves in the romantic idea of knights and damsels, of gallant gentlemen who knew how to treat a lady.

"The room has been cleaned and aired in preparation for your arrival." Fabian strode over to the oak bookcase. "I assume you read. The books may not be to your taste, but speak to Mackenzie, and he'll purchase whatever you need. If you'd like a frame and threads, I can have them sent from the mainland, too. The few female servants who work here only possess the tools to darn stockings."

She glanced at the door connecting her chamber to Fabian's suite. "Are you keeping me close because you fear I might run away?"

He pushed his hands through his hair, brushing it back off his shoulders, and the beginnings of a smile touched his lips. "I'm keeping you close for a variety of reasons."

The heat in his tone made her cheeks flame. Surely he didn't expect her to share his bed. "You said if we married I would be free to make my own decisions."

"Yes."

"What if I agree to your proposal but choose never to consummate our alliance?"

His mocking snort echoed through the chamber. "You want the truth, Lillian, and so I shall refrain from spouting flowery words of sentiment. The only hope I have of controlling Vane is through you. If we're married, and I mean in every sense that makes our partnership legal, he cannot take you away from here."

Her bruised heart screamed for her to run from Fabian Darcy, as far away as her tired legs could carry her. What good could come from a loveless marriage? But her logical brain saw the sense in forming an alliance. Though Vane swore otherwise, she was a burden to him. A guilty reminder of every mistake he'd ever made. The passage of time made matters worse. His need to atone meant he rarely let her out of his sight. If either of them had any chance of finding happiness, something had to change.

Marrying Fabian might not save her, but it would give Vane his freedom. She would just have to hope and pray her brother forgave her.

"If I'm to remain here, I have a list of demands."

"I expected nothing less."

Lillian folded her arms across her chest. "I have no use for frames and threads. To secure my co-operation, I want a rapier, sharpened, preferably with a bowl hilt. I want a pair of silver-mounted duelling pistols, preferably John Twigg and in a mahogany case."

For the first time in their long history, Fabian appeared shocked. "You don't need an armoury to protect yourself from me. I only take willing women to my bed."

The thought of him carousing and frolicking with tavern wenches caused an odd tightening in her chest. "If I'm to live amongst seafaring men, I insist on having a means of protection."

"It is one thing to own weapons, quite another to use them effectively. I would be foolish to grant such a request."

Lillian suppressed a smirk. She could shoot a target from a hundred yards, fence with skill, too. After the incident with Lord Martin, Vane insisted upon it. "Then I'm thankful my betrothed has granted me the freedom to make my own choices."

"Does that mean you accept my proposal?"

Lillian closed her eyes briefly and said a silent prayer. "If it means we might find Estelle alive, then yes, Fabian, I'll marry you."

"Is that the only reason?"

She didn't want to acknowledge the odd fluttering in her chest whenever he came near. This was a marriage of necessity ... a marriage of minds, nothing more.

"Yes, that's the only reason," she whispered, hoping he'd failed to detect the hitch in her voice, the telltale sound that said she was lying.

CHAPTER FOUR

F abian left Lillian in her bedchamber, closed the door and paused in the dimly lit corridor. He resisted the urge to punch the air triumphantly. Events were proceeding as planned. Once they were wed, he'd make sure Vane knew where to find them. The marquess would do anything to secure his sister's happiness. He would agree to help in the search for Estelle, and they stood a better chance of finding her if they worked together.

The need to save Estelle had forced him to harden his heart to all emotion. Marriage was nothing more than a business transaction—a case of bartering and exchanging commodities. So why was his pulse racing? Why did every nerve in his body spark to life at the thought of making Lillian Sandford his wife?

In his dreams, he'd asked her to marry him once before. He'd taken her to the orangery at Prescott Hall, proposed amid exotic flowers, promised to show her the world—not kidnap and blackmail her into submission. She'd smiled at him, not the scornful smirk she'd given tonight, but an expression of affection and respect. And the rightness of it all had penetrated deep into his soul.

But Fate had other plans.

Her father's greed and her brother's selfish pride had helped to dampen his desire. But while her acceptance to partake in his plan brought a sense of relief, it reawakened feelings long since buried. The powerful tug in his gut upon seeing her again was a testament to that.

Damn.

Sleep would elude him tonight. How could he rest knowing Lillian lay but a few feet beyond his bedchamber door? With a huff of frustration, he made his way to the kitchen. A man with Mackenzie's appetite and size would be filling his face.

"You'll find him in the brewery, my lord." Mrs Bell wiped her hands on her apron. "He treats those kegs like they're his children. Happen he's covering them with a blanket and singing a sweet lullaby."

Fabian laughed. "If I find him pushing one around in a perambulator, then I'll worry."

Mackenzie wasn't singing to the beer barrels, but Fabian found him sitting on a milking stool, one arm draped over a keg while he supped from a tankard.

"After a night out in the cold, I thought you'd be in the kitchen or nestled in a chair in front of a roaring fire."

"It's a matter of priorities, my lord." Mackenzie came to his feet. "This stuff needs drinking before it turns sour. Can I interest you in a mug of ale?"

"I'd rather a bottle of claret, but I'll take whatever's going tonight." He needed something to banish all amorous thoughts of the woman in the adjoining chamber.

Mackenzie placed his tankard on the stool, rummaged around on the shelf to his right, blew dust from an earthenware mug and filled it from the tap in the keg.

Drinks in hand they clinked vessels in salute.

"To the best-laid plans," Fabian said.

"Aye, even if they're not the most moral ones." Mackenzie gave a weary sigh. "How's the lass faring?"

"Better than expected. This time tomorrow she'll be my wife." Fabian clutched the mug and hoped Mackenzie didn't notice the slight tremble in his fingers. "Please tell me you brought the Reverend Sykes with you."

"Aye, we've brought the minister. He made a bit of a fuss. Tried to tell me you should marry on the mainland. As it turns out, the man's a poor sailor and spent his time aboard casting up his accounts."

Despite being five miles from shore, Raven Island was part of the parish of Branscombe in the county of Devonshire. Whether he liked it or not, the reverend had a duty to serve all his parishioners.

"Granted, no one has used the old chapel in a hundred years, but the Reverend Sykes cannot refuse to attend us here."

Mackenzie swallowed a mouthful of ale and wiped his mouth with the back of his hand. "Och, he soon saw sense when I gave him your generous donation to fix the leaking roof. He wanted to see proof of your common licence, mind, but I told him no one questions the word of the Raven."

"I trust Isaac found him a comfortable room for the night?"

"Aye, though I'd best tell the reverend the ceremony is in the morning." Mackenzie frowned. "I thought the lass would want more time to prepare, though I'm surprised she agreed to the match at all."

"The lady has few options it seems." A sharp stab in his chest forced him to curse the man responsible. "Blast Vane. I could string him up for his failure to care for her as he should." The Lillian Sandford he remembered deserved to marry a duke, not a pirate. "We cannot afford to wait. Vane is a man of many talents. Let's hope hunting isn't one of them."

"You need tracks to hunt. Those at Vauxhall were too eager to escape being hit by a giant basket to notice us. We paid a few of Mr Green's men to cause a distraction."

"And you're certain Vane didn't follow you?"

"Aye." Mackenzie gave a hearty belch before refilling his tankard from the tap. "Trevane got caught up in the crowd. The gardens are too vast for one man to search alone."

"What about the other man you hired to help? You know I would have advised against it had you told me of your plans." One could not buy loyalty. His men knew that. "Are you assured of his discretion?"

"The other man, my lord?"

"The one whose face is pitted with smallpox scars. Lady Lillian said he frightened her out of her wits."

Mackenzie drew his bushy brows together and shook his head. "We know better than to hire a stranger. The lass is mistaken. Happen the laudanum made her confused."

"Perhaps." The hairs on Fabian's neck prickled to attention. After eight years at sea, he'd learnt to trust his intuition. "And you befriended no one during your stay in London?"

"Other than the odd conversation with the landlord of the Eight Bells, we kept to ourselves." Mackenzie placed his tankard on the milking stool and straightened. "But on a different note, there is something you should know, though you'll be none too pleased."

Fabian swallowed. "Is that why you've been plying me with ale?"

"Happen it's wise to keep your temper, what with a man of God sleeping but a few feet above." Mackenzie drew in a deep breath. "Someone has been stealing food from the pantry. Small amounts, but often. Mrs Bell didn't want to worry you and so mentioned it to me."

When one lived and worked with a hundred or more seafaring men, trust was everything. "The men know to ask Mrs Bell for anything they need, and she would not refuse their request." Some of his men lived a mile north of the castle, in a settlement of stone cottages close to the dock. Fifty or so men were out on *The Octavia* transporting wine from Bordeaux to Bristol.

Mackenzie sighed. "It's not just food, but candles, a lamp and firewood, too."

"Bloody hell! Why didn't Mrs Bell mention it before?"

"I imagine she didn't want to trouble you until she was certain of her findings. I told her I would investigate the matter. In the meantime, I'd best warn her about the banquet tomorrow. She'll need all hands in the kitchen tonight if she's got any hope of cooking up a feast."

"The banquet?"

Mackenzie gripped Fabian's shoulder. "Your wedding banquet. Surely you plan to give the lass a day to remember."

In regard to the ceremony and the deflowering of his bride, Fabian's only thoughts were of getting the deed done before Vane arrived. But then he reminded himself that there wouldn't be a deflowering as he wasn't the first man to take the scandalous lady to his bed. His chest grew hot, and little lights flashed before his eyes. Curse Vane to the Devil. Curse the blighter who took advantage of an innocent woman. Curse him for using and discarding such a precious treasure.

"I'd not planned on doing anything to mark the occasion." After all, she didn't want to marry him. "I'm sure the lady wishes to get the matter over with quickly and with the minimal of fuss." While taking Lillian to his bed was a priority, he wanted to do his utmost to ensure she enjoyed the experience. He had no intention of leading a life of celibacy. And he would not be unfaithful to his wife.

"Mark my words, you'd best make an effort to do something special else it will come back to haunt you for the rest of your days."

Fabian snorted. "Ordinarily, that responsibility would fall to her family. As the person who clearly knows the workings of a woman's mind, I shall give you the task of ensuring the lady is happy."

Mackenzie raised his chin. "It would be my pleasure to see that the day goes smoothly. I trust the lass has a dress."

Damn. "Only the one she's wearing."

Mackenzie threw his hands in the air. "Lord of all the fairies, you did not think the matter through at all." He huffed and sighed, tugged his beard and shaped the wiry hair into a point. "My mother used to say a pretty face suits a dish-cloth, but I doubt she meant on a lass' wedding day. You should be thankful she's related to Trevane for she has grit and courage aplenty."

"The lady has always possessed a fighting spirit." In their youth, she'd climbed to the highest bough of a tree just to prove a point, had done her utmost to suppress her fear when she struggled to get down. "And she'll need one to marry me."

"Happen it will take a lot to unsettle the lass. Och, I'll gather a few of the women together and see what we can do about finding her something decent to wear. Let's hope and pray our mysterious thief hasn't stolen every needle and thread."

"Lady Lillian has a natural beauty." One glance at her hazel eyes and a man would crawl on hands and knees to do her bidding. "I'm certain she'll look presentable in whatever she wears."

"Presentable?" Mackenzie shook his head and tutted. "Whatever you do, don't say that to her. A Highland lass would knock you on your backside and banish you to the barn."

Mackenzie was so caught up in the romantic notion of it all he'd forgotten Fabian's was to be a marriage of convenience.

"Then I best heed your wise words. The lady asked for pistols and a rapier as wedding gifts."

Mackenzie's eyes widened, and he laughed so hard his

shoulders shook. "You've got your hands full there, make no mistake. Wait until the wee bairns come along, you'll not have a minute's peace."

"Bairns?" A man needed to bed his wife to sire offspring. Fabian had more chance of waking to find the point of a blade pricking his throat. "Hold that thought. The lady will need time to grow accustomed to her new situation."

"From what I can tell she's a strong-minded woman who's learnt to take things in her stride. I imagine she'll enjoy being mistress of Raven Island, and wife to the bravest man ever to sail the seas."

"Brave? After the scrapes we've been in, some would use the term *foolish*."

Mackenzie raised his tankard. "We've not lost a man yet."

That wasn't entirely true.

Doyle hadn't tumbled overboard. He'd not fallen off the topsail or been swept off the deck by a thirty-foot wave. But he was lost all the same: swallowed by greed.

"Have you heard from Doyle?" Fabian knew the answer. Mackenzie would have told him had the disloyal rogue made contact.

Mackenzie's expression darkened. "Not since the day he tried to murder his own shipmates. He knows better than to come begging and pleading to me."

"I thought he might send for Mary at the very least." Doyle's wife lived in a cottage near the dock. Despite Fabian's reassurance that she knew nothing of Doyle's deceit, the men were nervous around her. But Fabian refused to turn her out.

"The man thinks only of himself. Most would say she's better off without him."

Fabian downed a mouthful of ale while he contemplated Mackenzie's comment. "Has Mary approached Mrs Bell for provisions since Doyle's disappearance? Perhaps she's afraid to see the men after what happened. Perhaps someone in the castle is stealing food and delivering it to her."

"Mary's not a thief. I can vouch for that." Mackenzie frowned and drew his hand down his beard. "But I'll visit her after the wedding, see how she's faring and ask if she's heard from that traitorous bastard."

The mere mention of his wedding sent Fabian's blood racing through his veins. "I suppose I should visit Lillian in her chamber and tell her we're to marry in the morning."

"Och, you cannot do that. A man cannot see his bride the night before the nuptials."

Fabian suppressed a chuckle. "How else am I to inform her of the news?"

"You can do what all men with love in their hearts do when there's something important to say."

Love in his heart? Mackenzie had downed too much ale and taken to spouting gibberish. "And what would a man in love do?"

"Why, he'd send the lass a letter."

CHAPTER FIVE

"Wake up, my lady." The sweet whisper drifted past Lillian's ear. "Wake up, my lady. You're getting married this morning, and there's much to do."

Lillian shuffled onto her side and snuggled beneath the sheets, desperate to return to the dream where she commanded the fastest ship ever to sail the seven seas.

A gentle hand settled on her arm and rocked her back and forth. "Unless you want to marry in your shift, you'd best open your eyes."

A loud clatter and a woman's muttered curse dragged Lillian's mind to the present.

"Och, I asked you to fill the tub not empty the bucket over the damn floor." Mackenzie's deep voice echoed through the room. "Can you not follow simple orders?"

Good Lord! The Scot was in her bedchamber.

"You're not aboard your ship now, Mackenzie," a woman shouted. "Get out of here, you daft oaf. A man cannot enter a lady's bedchamber unless he's her husband. This ain't the Highlands."

"And it ain't one of those fancy houses in Bloomsbury,

neither. I promised his lordship I'd have the lass at the church on time and the Devil himself won't stop me."

Lillian watched the amusing scene through half-closed eyes.

A short woman in a mobcap and apron scuttled over and pushed the Scot in the chest. "I don't care where in the world we are. Get your no-good prying eyes out of here before I throw the next bucket over you."

"I should like to see you try."

Another woman, busy weaving roses around a twine wreath, chuckled. "You can come to my house tonight, Mackenzie, if you want to see a lady in her shift. My husband won't be back for a week or more, and it can get mighty cold in the cottage."

All the women in the room tittered.

The Scot's cheeks flushed red. "For the love of God, have you never heard of a man with honest intentions? Is it a crime to want the lass to have a special day?"

Lillian suppressed the urge to jump off the bed and throw her arms around Mackenzie's thick neck. It had been a long time since anyone other than Vane had given her a passing thought.

"Then unless you have experience with curling irons and pins, you should leave us to our business. There must be something else you can do."

"Aye." Mackenzie tutted. "Happen I can get someone to spruce up the pews. But I shall need the lady dressed and ready in the great hall by eleven o'clock."

"If you want us ready by eleven, you'd best go now." The short woman shooed him away. "The lady cannot rise from her bed while you're standing there ogling."

"Ogling? Och, you have a witch's tongue, Nancy Hill." Mackenzie threw his hands in the air and gave a resigned sigh. "Very well. I'll leave you to your duties. If you need anything, send word to the church."

Lillian waited until Mackenzie stomped from the room and

closed the door before she sat up. All the women stopped what they were doing and stared. Lillian was used to people gaping, used to sly smirks and spiteful sniggers. Yet these women gazed upon her with an air of wonder.

The short woman, who was half Mackenzie's size but more than a match for the fiery Scot, stepped forward. "Oh, my lady, you're awake."

Lillian smiled. "I doubt there is a person alive who could sleep through Mackenzie's deep rumbles."

"Oh, the man likes to pretend he's got a temper, but his heart is as soft as his head." The woman curtsied. "I'm Mrs Hill, but please call me Nancy. My husband, Joseph, captains *The Octavia* when the master's not aboard, and I attend to the housekeeping duties here." She gestured to the other women present. "This is Heather, Ida and Gail. Their husbands work for his lordship, too."

All the women stepped forward and curtsied.

"The girl at your bedside is Penny," Nancy continued.

Penny held the edges of her apron and dipped a curtsy. "My father takes care of the stables, and I work as a maid here in the castle." The girl looked no older than sixteen. With red hair and freckles aplenty, she appeared far too innocent to attend to a crew of seafaring men.

"And I'm Ursula." A buxom wench with golden hair stepped forward. She walked with an exaggerated sway of the hips, a ploy often used by courtesans to flaunt their wares. Then again, after her scandalous encounter with Lord Martin, Lillian was ill-equipped to judge a person's morals. "I'm to be your maid, my lady, if you'll have me."

"Forgive me, m-my lady," Nancy stuttered. "I expect you're used to choosing your own staff, but here good girls are scarce. Ursula's the only one who knows how to style a lady's hair, having once worked in a fancy house in London."

Lillian didn't need a maid. Fabian promised her a life without fuss. It was one of the many reasons she'd accepted his proposal. But as a lady trained to run a large house, she knew the value of good relationships with one's staff.

"I'm grateful to you all and welcome your help."

"Perhaps tomorrow I could give you a tour of the castle and introduce you to the staff. That's if you're of a mind to leave the master's bed." Nancy slapped her hand over her mouth. Her eyes grew so wide her lashes almost touched her brows. "Oh, Lord, I didn't mean to say that aloud."

Ursula shook her head. "You must forgive our crude ways, my lady. We're used to speaking as we please and forget to mind our tongues."

"In truth, I find your honesty refreshing." She'd had a gutful of lies and deceit, of fake smiles and cruel whispers. "You may speak freely and know that I shall do the same."

With a collective exhale of breath, the women's shoulders relaxed.

"Then we need to get you into the tub if we've any hope of having you ready by eleven." Nancy beckoned Lillian from the bed. "I know if I were marrying Lord Ravenscroft I'd be darting about like a March hare."

The women sighed as though the man in question was the most coveted of the species, not a kidnapper using an innocent woman to his own end.

The sudden thought that this was her wedding day caused a flurry of mixed emotions. For a few precious seconds, her heart swelled. She had expected to live a lonely existence, to die a spinster. Ten years ago, she'd have given anything to marry Fabian. If only she could rouse the same sense of excitement she experienced then. But it was hopeless. Inside she was a hollow cavern, a dark empty place long since abandoned.

"If I were marrying Lord Ravenscroft, I'd save my energy," Heather said with a chuckle.

Lillian's stomach flipped, and her blood raced hot through her veins. "Lord Ravenscroft is the one who'll need to conserve his energy." Oh, he'd have to do some chasing if he hoped to lure her to his bed.

"We'll all need the strength of a saint if we're not ready to meet Mackenzie." Nancy came over to the bed and offered her hand. "Come, my lady. Time is of the essence as they say."

The next hour passed by in a blur. Lillian clutched the locket in her palm for fear of getting it wet as she slid into the tub. Numerous times Nancy advised her to remove it but she needed it today more than ever. With no time to wash and dry her hair, Ursula sprayed it with rosewater, curled and pinned it into a simple chignon. The silk dress she'd worn to Vauxhall had vanished. No doubt someone had the task of pressing out the creases and wiping mud off the hem.

Nancy hurried into the room carrying a different dress. "This one is nowhere near as pretty as the one you'd choose yourself." She held the garment aloft. "But it's new and will fit you like a glove."

The high-waisted morning dress in pale muslin was a shade lighter than peach, a shade darker than ivory. The only adornment consisted of a length of orange ribbon tied beneath the bosom.

The hairs on her neck prickled. Had Fabian been so confident in his skills of persuasion that he'd already purchased a wedding outfit? "Is this the dress Lord Ravenscroft wishes me to wear?" She could not keep the disdain from her voice. For a man who promised freedom, he took control of every situation.

"His lordship made no mention of a dress," Nancy said. "Mackenzie found this in one of the chests given to Lord Ravenscroft after his last voyage. Merchants often offer a bounty if their goods arrive on time."

Once again, it was Mackenzie who had her best interests at

heart. Fabian wouldn't care if she married him wearing nothing but her chemise.

"There's a string of pearls that would look pretty draped around your fine neck."

Lillian stroked her locket. "I've no need for jewels."

Nancy pursed her lips as her gaze drifted to the gold necklace, but she said nothing.

The women set about dressing her. Ursula tugged the ties on her corset as though hauling a hundred fish in a net.

"Not too tight else I'm liable to swoon."

"If Lord Ravenscroft were waiting at the altar for me, I'd swoon," Heather said with a giggle. "And I'd get there an hour early in case he thought to change his mind."

Why would Fabian change his mind when her co-operation was part of his plan?

With care, Nancy and Ida lifted the dress over her head. They brushed and fiddled with the material until it covered her body like a second skin. Ursula slid the orange length of satin around Lillian's waist and cinched it tight under the bosom.

They all stepped back and surveyed their work.

"Oh, there's a pretty red and gold shawl." Nancy scuttled over to the chair and returned with the square of silk. "I don't suppose it will keep out the cold, but it will complement your dark hair."

The women fussed over her for another few minutes before escorting her down to the great hall.

The thud of Mackenzie's boots, as he paced the flagstones, echoed through the dank corridor. He swung around upon hearing their approach and glared at Nancy. "Can you not tell the time, woman? You're ten minutes late."

"Oh, silly me," Nancy retorted. "I forgot to check my pocket watch."

Mackenzie tutted, but as his gaze fell to Lillian, he clutched his chest. "Praise be, you're a sight to behold, lass."

Nancy huffed. "You can't be calling the mistress of the house *lass*."

"Och, I mean no disrespect." He bowed. "Forgive me, my lady, for my heathen ways. A lifetime aboard a ship can rid a man of all sense of propriety."

"Don't you mean it can rid a man of all sense?" Nancy said.

The other women grinned.

"You're forgiven, Mackenzie," Lillian said. His tone brimmed with warmth when he called her *lass*. There was something genuine and honest about him, dare she say trustworthy. "You may call me *lass* in private. When we've company, you'd best call me *my lady*."

The man's fiery beard twitched as he smiled and puffed his chest. "Thank you, my lady."

"I trust his lordship is waiting at the church." Lillian hadn't spoken to Fabian since she'd agreed to marry him. He'd not bothered to inform her personally that she had but hours to prepare for the wedding, but instead had pushed a note under her door. She'd spent the night tossing and turning, mulling over her decision. Would she find the courage to make the declaration before God?

"His lordship is out riding, my lady, and has been gone all morning." Mackenzie squirmed on the spot, and his cheeks flamed. "He'll be here for the service. You can be sure of that."

Would he? Fabian's contempt for her family knew no bounds.

Lillian snorted in an attempt to ease the sharp stab in her chest. It was foolish to expect Fabian to show her the same consideration he had in his youth. Now he was a man of numerous identities: lord of the seas, a pirate, the Raven. The ceremony was a mere formality. A union of necessity. She'd spent the morning doing her utmost to look her best. No doubt Fabian would turn up splattered in mud, wearing the crumpled clothes he'd slept in the night before.

"Perhaps we should wait until his lordship returns." Lillian feigned a smile. "I see little point riding to the church when in all likelihood he might change his mind."

Mackenzie frowned. "When Lord Ravenscroft makes a promise, you can be certain he'll keep it." Admiration and respect filled the Scot's voice. "His lordship will be at the church. I'll stake my life on it."

Mackenzie's comment went some way to restoring her faith in Lord Ravenscroft. When a man commanded the respect of his people, he was obviously doing something right.

"Then you may escort me to my carriage," Lillian said with a teasing grin.

"Carriage?" Mackenzie struggled to look her in the eye. "I'm afraid the best we can do is a horse and cart, my lady."

Lillian did chuckle then. If she didn't laugh, she might cry. "Do I get to ride up front or am I to sit with the turnips?"

"Come with me, my lady." Mackenzie led them out into the bailey. "I'm happy to say there's not a turnip in sight."

"I think you'll like what they've done," Penny said, clapping her hands as she skipped at Lillian's side. "My parents spent all morning getting it ready."

The sight of the decorated cart brought them all to an abrupt halt. The smartly dressed man perched on the seat wore a green coat and top hat. Next to him, a red velvet cushion with gold tassels marked the spot where Lillian should sit. Thick swags of green foliage threaded with pink roses hung from the sides of the cart.

"It's beautiful, Mackenzie." Lillian looked up at him and offered a beaming grin.

"The Browns deserve the credit. I just told them to make it pretty." Mackenzie walked over to the cart and held out his hand. "Let me help you, my lady. We'd best be on our way if we want to arrive on time."

Lillian climbed up and sat on the padded cushion. The women were all set to wave her off until Mackenzie told them to remove their mobcaps and aprons and climb into the back of the cart.

A flurry of excitement erupted as the women set about straightening their hair and clothes. Penny rushed to fetch her mother, who appeared looking confused and dazed.

Once they were all inside the cart, it rattled out of the bailey, through the gatehouse and along a narrow road running parallel with the cliff edge. The sight of the sea had a calming effect, and the women's raucous laughter proved infectious.

"Are you touching my leg, Malcolm Mackenzie?" Heather teased.

"Is that your way of asking if I will?" Mackenzie replied with a hearty chuckle. "Because if it's all the same, I'd rather keep my fingers." A collective gasp left the Scot stuttering. "What I ... what I mean is your husband will chop off every digit if he thinks I've made him a cuckold."

"I reckon he'd chop off more than your fingers," Mr Brown called back over his shoulder.

Everyone laughed until they cried. Lillian could not remember the last time she had raised more than a smile. She'd been at the castle for less than a day, and yet these wonderful, honest people had found a way into her heart.

She sat on the plush cushion, a grin stretching from ear to ear, until the sight of the church in the distance sent her nerves scattering like leaves in a storm. The quaint stone building was a solid reminder of all she'd promised. Not love or companionship, just her assistance.

Panic flared.

She should turn back, find a boat and row for the mainland. But her lonely life in London was a poor one indeed. And she needed to set Vane free for him to have any chance of happiness.

"I'll help you down, my lady, and then I'll go inside and see if they're ready." Mackenzie's words broke her reverie.

Lillian forced a smile and was grateful for the Scot's firm grip, as her knees almost buckled when her feet touched the ground. "Thank you, Mackenzie. Thank you for everything."

The man bent his head and whispered, "You're welcome, lass."

Mackenzie strode off up the narrow path leading to the church's open door. The women gathered around Lillian, excitement palpable in the air.

Mackenzie returned, his lips drawn thin beneath his beard.

"What is it?" Lillian's heart skipped a beat. "Is the minister here?"

"Aye, the minister is inside, along with some of his lordship's men." Mackenzie exhaled deeply as he narrowed his gaze and scanned the coastal heathland.

One did not need to be skilled at reading minds to understand the problem. "Lord Ravenscroft is not here, is he?" Disappointment surfaced. Fabian had not lied to her, but anyone with an ounce of kindness in their heart would have made an effort, today of all days.

Mackenzie grimaced. "He'll be here any moment."

"Did you check his bed?" she mocked, but then remembered that Fabian had gone riding. Part of her wanted to make excuses for him. Had he taken a tumble, sprained an ankle?

"Never fear, my lady." Nancy placed a comforting hand on Lillian's arm. "His lordship is likely preening himself, eager to look his best."

Or more likely he'd arrive half-dressed, mumble his vows and disappear again.

The thud of horse's hooves pounding the ground caught Lillian's attention. A black stallion appeared on the brow of the hill. The beast galloped towards them, leaving a cloud of dust where its hooves struck the dirt. A silver sheen of sweat covered the animal's coat, and its look of determination mirrored that of its master.

Mackenzie exhaled. "Lord Ravenscroft likes to make a grand entrance that's for sure."

Not *so* grand, Lillian thought, for his muscular thighs were hidden beneath the folds of his greatcoat. Dressed as he was, anyone would think he'd ridden through the damp, foggy streets of London and not along the rugged coastline on a fresh summer's day.

Fabian came to a sliding stop before them. He gave his horse a reassuring pat before swinging down in one fluid movement.

Lillian swallowed hard as he strode towards her, dark and masterful. "How good of you to join us, my lord."

Everyone held their breath as they watched with wide, curious eyes.

Fabian ignored them all and kept his heated gaze fixed on her. "I beg your forgiveness." The rich tone of his voice sent her stomach skipping up to her chest. "An urgent matter commanded my attention."

No doubt many things mattered more than marrying her.

"I pray it was important enough to make you late on your wedding day."

The corners of his mouth curled into a half smile rather than down with shame. "You may judge for yourself."

He marched back to his horse, and the women took the opportunity to breathe. After reaching into his saddlebag, he returned with a small posy of flowers.

"Did you not tell me once that wild roses were your flower of choice?" He brought the posy to his nose and inhaled. "Did you not say you found the scent uplifting?"

He remembered.

Lillian's heart thumped against her ribs. He'd gone riding just to find her flowers? "I did."

Fabian handed her the posy. *"The rose looks fair, but fairer we it deem—"*

"For that sweet odour which doth in it live," she said, completing the line from Shakespeare's sonnet. Her fingers trembled as she accepted the small bouquet.

He stepped closer. "A person's inner worth enhances their outward beauty." His voice came in a soft, seductive whisper. "The rose is more beautiful because of its sweet scent. Equally, a woman's compassionate heart only adds to her appeal."

The words washed over her like the sun's warm rays. Still, when it came to displays of sentiment, she knew enough of men to err on the side of caution. "Is that your way of thanking me for helping you?"

"If I wanted to thank you, I would have simply said the words."

"So you're saying you admire my kind heart?" Her voice carried a hint of amusement. Compliments were hard to swallow.

"I am saying you're more beautiful to me because of it."

The comment robbed her of breath. Despite every effort, she couldn't help but gulp in air.

Fabian smiled. "Perhaps you're not used to men being so direct. But I speak the truth, Lillian. You've always known that." He stepped back, shrugged out of his greatcoat and handed the garment to Mackenzie who placed it in the cart.

She half expected to see him in a loose shirt and creased breeches, but the sight of him caused desire to unfurl like the first bud of spring. Dressed in a dark blue coat, starched cravat and gold embroidered waistcoat, the Raven looked every bit a lord of the London ballrooms. With his hair tied back in a queue, he still possessed the roguish air of a pirate. It was a look she couldn't help but find appealing.

"Now, I believe we've kept the reverend waiting long enough." He bowed gracefully and gestured to the path leading up to the church door. "Shall we?"

The last time she'd agreed to be a man's wife it ended in disaster, ruination and a broken heart that would never fully heal. Lillian had been to Hell, looked into the Devil's black eyes, felt the scorching flames sear her skin as he branded her a whore.

Though Lord Ravenscroft had committed numerous sins, he was by no means a devil. Somewhere there was good in him. Was the sweet posy in her hand not testament to that?

CHAPTER SIX

All chattering ceased when Fabian entered the small stone church that had stood on the clifftop for centuries. His men had patched the holes in the roof, chased away the bats and rebuilt the dry-stone wall. Over the years, many people had stood at the altar and exchanged vows. No doubt few had used bribery and coercion to woo the bride.

A sudden pang of guilt hit him hard in the chest.

He was the worst of rogues. He knew that. But Lillian would have a better life with him than the one she presently had in London. No one wanted to be the subject of scandalous gossip. No lady should have to look to the gutter for a suitor. In that respect, Lillian needed saving almost as much as Estelle.

Fabian bit back a chuckle as he strode down the aisle. Huddled together in the box pews, the doors draped in pretty rose garlands, sat twenty or more of the toughest sailors ever to sail the seas.

Had this been St George's in Hanover Square, the throng would smile and nod politely, not jeer, wink and offer wide toothless grins. Still, these loyal, hardworking men had helped him make his fortune, and Fabian would be forever in their debt.

"Bet girls in every port are weeping into their aprons today," one of them muttered as Fabian walked past. "Who'd have thought to see his lordship wed?"

"Happen his betrothed is a siren. Who else can lure a sane man from a calm sea to a rocky shore?"

"Isn't a siren half woman, half bird?"

"All the more reason why she's marrying the Raven."

Fabian paid them no heed as he stood before the reverend at the altar, his hands clasped behind his back. Sailors told tales and invented stories to relieve the monotony of spending endless months at sea. Besides, how could he offer a witty reply when his tongue felt thick and clumsy? How could he contradict them when he feared Lillian Sandford *did* possess a magical ability to make a man lose his mind?

The church door creaked open. Nancy Hill and the rest of the women slipped inside, offering whispered apologies as they shuffled into one of the box pews. Ursula smiled and raised a teasing brow. Thank the Lord he'd declined every offer she'd made to warm his bed. The woman had been persistent in her methods, but Fabian would never disrespect his position or his staff.

"I trust the bride is on her way, my lord?" The Reverend Sykes sneezed into his handkerchief and wiped his nose ten times despite the surrounding skin being red and raw. The fellow suffered from every ailment known to man. Gout in his toe made standing a painful affair. "Old buildings are a curse when one has a weak constitution."

"Rest assured. The lady is here." Well, he hoped she'd not persuaded Mackenzie to command a rowboat and ferry her back to the mainland.

A man in the crowd cleared his throat. They all shifted in their seats and craned their necks to gain the best view of the door.

The Reverend Sykes gestured for the congregation to stand

but the men were so keen to glimpse the siren who'd bewitched their master, it took some time before they obliged.

Lillian hovered in the doorway. Due to her brother's absence, Mackenzie took his place at her side. She gripped his arm and pasted a smile. The pretty posy in her hand shook. Anyone would think she was about to walk the plank and plunge into shark-infested waters.

What did he expect? She agreed to marry him because he'd made it hard for her to say no. She agreed to marry him because no one else had asked her. From what little he'd seen, she had given up all hope of finding happiness.

As she walked towards him, his chest grew as tight as his throat.

What the hell was wrong with him?

Her beauty stole his breath ... surely that was it. With her styled coiffure and simple yet elegant dress, she looked every bit a lady of the *ton* and not a naive girl who'd given away her greatest treasure on a whim.

Damn Vane.

Fabian mentally shook himself. Bitterness had no place in his heart—not today.

Lillian came to stand before him, and he smiled. Her bottom lip quivered as she forced a smile, too.

The need to ease her fears took hold, and he closed the gap between them and bent his head. "There's no need to look so terrified. All will be well."

"I only wish I could trust your word," she said so he alone could hear.

The comment cut deep, but he deserved nothing less.

The reverend addressed the congregation, but Fabian placed a reassuring hand on her arm. "I swear you will not regret your decision." And by God, he meant it.

Lillian remained silent. She focused on the reverend who, in his eagerness to leave the cold, wretched place, recited the relevant passage from the Bible. Numerous times during the ceremony her gaze fell to Fabian. Her cheeks flushed scarlet at the mention of joining and of satisfying carnal lusts. Fear flashed in her eyes when the reverend informed them that marriage was ordained for the procreation of children.

"*Ye will answer at the dreadful day of judgement when the secrets of all hearts shall be disclosed,*" the reverend preached.

Lillian touched the gold locket at her neck. Until now, it had not occurred to him to ask if she loved another, if she kept his likeness close to her heart. Why would it when love played no part in their bargain? Still, the thought created an uneasy feeling in the pit of his stomach.

No one made a sound when called to offer a reason why they should not be wed.

The reverend turned to him. "*Wilt thou love her, comfort her, honour and keep her in sickness and in health?*"

Fabian stared into her eyes. The vows had a profound effect on him. A rush of heat flooded his body. "I will." Heaven help him. His heart pounded wildly in his chest. His life flashed before his eyes, every deed, every trial and tribulation culminating into this life-changing moment.

But what did it mean?

"*Wilt thou obey him, and serve him, love, honour...*"

Lillian struggled to hold Fabian's gaze.

A prolonged silence filled the stone building.

The whole congregation watched her intently. Mouths fell open. Heads hung forward as they waited for her reply.

Lillian looked at the posy in her hand and sighed. She glanced at Mackenzie who smiled and gave a reassuring nod.

The Reverend Sykes cleared his throat.

Fabian willed her to answer. During all his dangerous encounters at sea, he'd never felt a fear like the one gripping him now. Without Lillian at his side, he had no hope of gaining Vane's help. But that was not the reason for his internal discomfort.

"I—I will." A deep exhale followed her declaration.

Fabian's shoulders relaxed. The collective sigh from those squashed into the pews mirrored his own sense of relief.

The rest of the ceremony passed by in a blur as Fabian struggled to address the odd feeling of contentment filling his chest. They held hands, and he wasn't sure whose fingers trembled. They pledged their troth, knelt in prayer.

"*Those whom God hath joined together let no man put asunder,*" the reverend said before proceeding to announce them, "*man and wife together.*"

Together.

He'd been alone for so damn long, perhaps that was what unnerved him.

Soon they were outside, swamped by well-wishers cheering and shouting congratulations. The women stepped forward, grabbed a handful of petals from Nancy's basket and threw them in the air.

Lillian clutched Fabian's arm, and a sudden urge to protect her took hold.

Damnation. It wasn't supposed to be like this.

The celebratory cries proved infectious. A chuckle burst from Lillian's lips, the sound sweet, light-hearted, and then they were both smiling and laughing, both lost in a moment of pure bliss.

"Let me be the first to call you Lady Ravenscroft." Mackenzie came before them and bowed his head. "Mrs Bell has prepared a feast to mark the occasion. It won't be as grand as a wedding breakfast you'd have in London, mind, but it will be the best meal ever to grace our table."

Fabian turned to her. "When he says it won't be grand, he means we'll be dining with the men. Although if you prefer privacy, I can arrange for us to dine in the drawing room or my chamber." His mind chose that moment to imagine a feast of a different sort. One where her lips tasted of wild berries, and her skin tasted of milk and honey.

Lillian scanned the crowd and smiled. "No, I should like to hear their kind words and watch them drink a toast in our honour."

Clearly, the lady had never witnessed the bawdy antics of drunken sailors. When the ale flowed freely, things invariably became boisterous. "I cannot promise they'll mind their manners. These men do not live by the same rules of etiquette and decorum."

"Have no fear." Mackenzie puffed his chest. "I'll banish them to the dungeons for a night if they dare speak out of turn. I shall see to it personally."

"There are dungeons?" Lillian sounded surprised.

"Yes, though we've not had cause to use them—yet," Fabian teased. "I shall give you a tour of the castle this evening as long as you promise not to chain me up and leave me to rot."

"No doubt I would return in the morning to find you had escaped. If there is one thing I know about you, it's that you're resourceful."

The compliment touched him. It had taken years to come to terms with losing Prescott Hall. Quick wit and ingenuity had set him on the right path again.

Mackenzie cleared his throat. "I should head back. Mrs Bell threatened to spoil my ale unless I agreed to play footman."

Mackenzie climbed onto the seat next to Mr Brown, and the women clambered into the back of the cart. The men began their march towards the castle, eager to sample Mackenzie's prized ale before he drained the barrel.

"As my wife, you're expected to ride back with me." Fabian sensed her uncertainty. "Thunder is a little temperamental, but I recall you always favoured a spirited animal. Is that not another reason you agreed to marry me?"

"You called your horse Thunder?" She offered him a smirk.

"The name conveys strength and power, does it not? Is a man's horse not an extension of his character?"

Lillian's eyes lit up. "Indeed, you're a man of many contradictions, much like your horse." When Fabian frowned, she added, "Thunder looks rather timid with flowers tucked into his bridle."

Fabian swung around. Someone had pushed roses around the browband and headpiece, so it looked as though the beast wore a crown of flowers. "Blast Mackenzie. This is his doing."

Lillian pursed her lips. "I think he feels guilty for plying me with laudanum and stealing me away from home. He's doing everything he can to make me feel welcome, and to make this a special day."

The comment showed Fabian to be hopelessly inadequate. There wasn't a man alive with a heart as huge as Mackenzie's. What hope had he of making a good impression? Why did he even want to? "Be prepared for more surprises. Heaven knows what he's done to the great hall. Had I given him more time I'm sure he would have sewn petals into shoes and carved leaves into the wooden tables."

Lillian chuckled.

He liked it when her eyes shone with amusement. It reminded him of the carefree days of their youth. Noting the pink petal caught in her hair, he reached up to pluck it out. His fingers slipped into the silky strands, and he couldn't resist stroking her temple and cupping her cheek.

Lillian's eyelids fluttered, and she tilted her head a fraction as if leaning into his touch. But then she straightened and stepped back.

"We were friends once," he said. "Under the circumstances,

do you not think it wise to try again?" Friends and occasional lovers was the best he could hope for. Once Vane arrived, she would have an ally, someone to sour her opinion, someone to think for her.

Lillian remained silent for a moment. "Are the odds not stacked against us?"

She was probably right. She'd sacrificed her soul for Estelle, for peace and freedom.

"If I've learnt anything at sea, it's that this moment is all that matters. A sailor focuses on the destination at his peril."

"You mean one cannot expect to arrive at an idyllic location without effort." She brought the posy of flowers up to her nose and inhaled.

"No, we must work hard even if the journey is perilous, even if we want to abandon all hope and turn back."

"And where will our travels take us, do you think?"

He shrugged because he dared not think that far ahead. "There are havens littered along the coast." Places called Friendship, Respect and Love. "Let us hope the wind steers us on the right course."

"And what do we do when the storm comes?" Was she referring to Vane's imminent arrival? "Because it is coming, Fabian, make no mistake about that."

"Then we shall just have to weather it, and hope we're strong enough to stay afloat."

Something he said seemed to soothe her. Those bewitching hazel eyes softened, and she whispered, "Hope is all we have."

CHAPTER SEVEN

They rode back to the castle in silence. The sea breeze picked up momentum, and the temperature dropped. Lillian wrapped the shawl around her shoulders, and Fabian cursed for not having the foresight to remove his greatcoat from the cart.

"Lean into me. It will keep the wind off your back."

"I'm fine." She held her body rigid, inches away from him, as if he carried an infectious disease and the merest touch would cause certain death.

He leant forward and firmed his grip on the reins. Trapped in his arms, she had no choice but to rest against him. After a few muttered groans, she relaxed. He would have to take his time with her in bed. While a fiery passion simmered beneath the surface, it was clear she fought to suppress her feelings. Perhaps it had something to do with her scandalous past. Perhaps she despised him. But then he'd seen the flash of affection in her eyes when he'd given her the bouquet, one he'd seen many times in their youth.

They rode into the bailey to find Mackenzie swigging from his pocket flask while he waited. Alerted by the pounding of

Thunder's hooves, the Scot quickly replaced the top and slipped the flask into his pocket.

"I was hoping you'd be a wee while longer." Mackenzie gave a sly wink and then strode over and helped Lillian to the ground. "We're almost ready. Come, my lady."

A groom rushed to take Fabian's horse, eager to tend to the animal so he might partake in the festivities.

Fabian dismounted and brushed the dust from his coat. "I expected to find a carpet of crimson petals awaiting us."

"And you'd have had one if we had an endless supply of roses."

Fabian offered Lillian his arm, and she placed a tentative hand in the crook. Whenever she touched him, his heart fluttered about like a wild bird in a cage. Lord, he'd have to get these strange emotions under control.

They followed a grinning Mackenzie into the castle, stopped at the large oak doors and gave a collective gasp at the sight greeting them.

Like a hive in the height of summer, the great hall buzzed with activity.

His men dashed about, brought in platters of meats, bread and cheese, and placed them on the long tables. One table ran along the width of the dais. Two further tables ran the length of the great hall. All the candles glowed in the wall sconces. The fire in the stone hearth roared, the flames dancing in celebration, too.

The women laughed and hummed tunes as they brought in vases of flowers and flagons of wine and ale. Some had a light skip in their step as they went about their work. Excitement thrummed in the air.

Mackenzie stepped forward and gestured to the table on the dais and to the two throne chairs in the centre. "My lord, my lady. Please take your seats for the banquet."

Fabian stared at his friend and raised a brow. "Are you feeling well, Mackenzie?" He noticed one of his men setting up a music stand near the door while another drew his bow across the strings of a fiddle. The itch to accompany them proved great. "There are a few matrons in London who could use your skill for organising a party."

Mackenzie chuckled. "Fools make feasts, and wise men eat them. That's how it works in the Highlands though I fear you have the company of simple folk today."

"If you can arrange a banquet in less than a day," Lillian said with some amazement, "what could you achieve if given a week?"

"Allow me to warn my mistress that a Scot will take up any challenge when he's had a drink." Mackenzie inclined his head respectfully but tapped his finger to his nose and winked. "I have a few surprises in store for tomorrow."

Fabian groaned inwardly. "I think you've enough to concern yourself with for now." Catching the thief was the priority. Not because he cared about losing food and provisions. Trust and loyalty mattered more to him than money.

With the tables overladen with platters of food, everyone waited for Fabian and Lillian to take their seats before finding a spot on a bench. Soon the great hall was alive with boisterous chatter, salutes and cheers. Clearly, Mackenzie had given strict orders when it came to dining in front of a lady. His men ate with cutlery. They sipped their ale as opposed to emptying the vessel in one gulp. Freddie wiped his mouth with a napkin and not his shirt sleeves. But Fabian wasn't the only one impressed with their manners.

"I must say I find your men rather civil." Lillian placed her wine glass on the table and turned to him. "Where do they live when not at sea? Surely not in the castle."

Fabian bit back a chuckle. Was that her way of reminding him she needed pistols? "Over a hundred men work for me."

"A hundred?"

It took fifty men working together to sail a merchant ship and transport cargo. "There are but two dozen here at any one time. Most of them live in the cottages near the dock. The unmarried men share accommodation. Mackenzie is the only one who resides here." Because he was the only man in the world Fabian trusted.

Lillian glanced at Mackenzie seated at the end of their table. "Your friend is a remarkable man, that is when he's not kidnapping innocent women from the Pleasure Gardens."

"He's old enough to be your father." Jealousy crawled through Fabian's veins. Would she ever use the word *remarkable* to describe him? "What I mean is he takes the role of protector seriously. It was out of loyalty to me that he behaved as he did at Vauxhall."

A vision of her wearing her pretty lavender dress flashed into his mind, of her laughing and dancing as gentlemen bombarded her with attention. After enjoying the company of high society, now she dined with men who thought salt pork a delicacy.

"I should despise him," she said. "Drugging a woman is not what one would consider gentlemanly. And yet I cannot help but like him."

"And what about me? Do you like me, Lillian? Am I forgiven for stealing you away from everything you hold dear?"

A dark sadness settled over her face. She fought back the few tears filling her eyes. The sight cut him deep. By God, he felt like the worst of scoundrels. He had not thought this plan through at all.

"I have always liked you, Fabian. Though I do not always agree with your methods or principles."

"Believe me when I tell you, I wish there had been some other way of achieving my goal."

"So you wish you could have saved Estelle without marrying

me?" The tremor in her voice revealed an inner pain, and she struggled to hold his gaze. Ironically, he didn't want to hurt her—he'd never wanted that. From the moment he'd uttered the words *I will*, the overwhelming need to make her happy consumed him.

"That is not what I said. I mean things might have been different if we had married under the right circumstances." Part of him wished to eradicate the last eight years, although Vane would never have permitted her to marry a man verging on bankruptcy.

Their conversation was cut short by Mackenzie who'd found a gavel and sound block from somewhere, the thud of the wooden hammer capturing everyone's attention.

"The men insist on doing something to mark the occasion." Mackenzie hammered his gavel again when the sailors jeered and taunted their shipmates. "If it pleases my lord and lady, may I present the first of the day's entertainment."

Fabian could not prevent the wide grin from forming. Mackenzie was worth more than his hefty weight in gold. He gave a nod of approval and turned to Lillian. "Don't expect to see skill like that of Madame Pesqui, the tightrope walker. These men are likely to fall off a plank after supping Mackenzie's ale."

Lillian's smile replaced the solemn expression she had worn moments earlier. For that, he owed Mackenzie another debt of gratitude.

"Allow me to present Skinny Malinky." Mackenzie gestured for the man to come and take the floor as the musicians in the corner of the room struck a few chords on their fiddles.

"Skinny Malinky?" Lillian screwed up her nose. "What an odd name."

"Apparently it's a Scottish term. Alfred has extremely long legs as I believe he is about to demonstrate."

The fellow came forward, bowed to them and performed an odd folk dance that saw him whipping his long limbs up high in the air. His shipmates gasped and ducked for fear of being kicked as Skinny jigged about in the space between the long tables.

Next, came Freddie Fortune, a man known for being sleight of hand. With permission, he approached the dais. Lillian picked a playing card from a dog-eared pack. After sliding the card back into the deck without anyone seeing it, Freddie shuffled and threw some onto the floor before plucking the correct card from behind Lillian's ear.

With his eyes trained on her every expression, Fabian experienced a sudden rush of warmth to his chest whenever she giggled.

"How on earth did he do that?" In her excitement, she clutched Fabian's arm and the heat plaguing his body warmed another part of his anatomy.

"He has plenty more tricks up his sleeve if you pardon the pun."

The festivities continued. Isaac juggled apples, much to Mrs Bell's annoyance. The women came together and sang an old country tune: a heartrending tale of a sailor separated from his one true love.

Lillian sniffed numerous times, dabbed her eyes and sipped her wine. When the song came to an end, she breathed a sigh of relief, and he couldn't help but feel she had a lost love somewhere.

His gaze drifted to the locket at her throat, and he fought the urge to ask to see the portrait of the gentleman inside.

After listening to a tune played on glass bottles, Fabian glanced at Mackenzie. "And what have you next, an imp who can raise snakes from a basket?"

Mackenzie chuckled. "From the breadth of your chest, I'd say you're no imp, my lord, and some might say you make a noise loud enough to send the snakes slithering." Mackenzie reached under the table and produced a fiddle.

Lord, no! "Surely you don't expect me to play on my wedding day?"

"Aye, I imagine your bride would like to witness your skill with a bow."

Lillian touched his arm again. "Please play for me, Fabian."

He met her gaze. What was it about those enchanting hazel eyes that made a man eager to do her bidding? How the hell could he refuse?

Fabian pushed out of his throne chair. "Very well. But if I'm to play, then you will all dance." He held out his hand to Lillian. "Come. Mackenzie will partner you, though you must follow his lead. I've tried to teach them various dances over the years, but the men have trouble following routine steps. Indeed, I doubt their movements will resemble any dances you know."

Her eyes brightened as she placed her hand in his. "You mean there's no one here to berate me for a misstep?"

"I told you, no one here will judge you." For some unknown reason, he bent his head and brushed his lips over her knuckles. "You're free to do whatever you please."

"Then lead the way, my lord."

While the men set about finding a woman to partner, Fabian left Lillian in Mackenzie's capable hands. Mackenzie tapped a tune with his foot and twirled Lillian around as he tried to explain the basic moves of the dance. Fabian warmed up his fiddle by performing a series of short bows on each string, though the task proved difficult when his wife's chuckles drew his attention.

The sound of the first few chords forced the crowd to stop their antics and fix their gazes on him. Fabian's heart pounded in his throat. Not because he doubted his skill for playing and entertaining, but when Lillian stared at him, he glimpsed a look of wonder and admiration flashing in her eyes.

Mackenzie bowed to Lillian, took her hand and then the ten or so couples took to moving in time to the music. The steps were more akin to excited leaps and skips than any set pattern. They linked arms, swung each other around until dizzy. Their breathless chuckles were the perfect accompaniment to his tune.

"Make a circle," Mackenzie shouted, and everyone rushed to find their place and grab their neighbour's shoulder.

The faster Fabian played, the quicker their feet shuffled around and around the flagstone floor. Fabian watched Lillian. His wife laughed until she couldn't catch her breath. A few locks of ebony hair came loose from her coiffure to bounce at her flushed cheeks. The muscles in his abdomen tightened, unfulfilled lust leaving a heavy ache in his groin.

Lord, had he expected to marry her and feel nothing?

Eyes wide with exhilaration, her gaze met his. Like a bolt from the heavens, the power of it made him play the wrong note. In the midst of their merriment, no one noticed. Still, in his eagerness to gain his wife's attention, he skipped to the end and stroked his last note.

Everyone clapped and cheered, oblivious to his selfish act.

Lillian touched Mackenzie on the upper arm in a gesture of appreciation. Fabian strode over to them, weaving through the crowd who rewarded his efforts with a cheer or a curtsy.

"You were remarkable." Lillian's vibrant eyes settled on him. Only moments earlier he'd wished he was worthy of her esteem. And yet her praise wasn't enough to satisfy the clawing need within.

"When one spends months aboard a ship, one must find something to do of an evening." What might his nights have been like had he returned to his cabin to find Lillian waiting for him in bed? "Perhaps you might care to join me on my next voyage."

"Perhaps."

The brief silence made him acutely aware of his own erratic heartbeat thumping in his ears.

She placed her hand on her chest, the rapid rise and fall drew his gaze. "Heavens, I think I need to rest. It's been an age since I've danced."

"I doubt you've ever danced like that."

A chuckle escaped. "You're right, though I would rather a folk dance than the rigid, stifled steps one sees in the ballroom."

"I don't think I've ever seen you laugh so hard." For a reason unbeknown, a lump formed his throat, and he turned to Mackenzie by way of a distraction. "You've outdone yourself, my friend."

"The day's not over yet, my lord."

They returned to their seats on the dais. Lillian's breath still came in ragged pants, and he couldn't help but imagine a similar sound breezing past his ear as he thrust into her warm, welcoming body.

Willie Wright, the only man ever to wear his hair in braids, stepped forward. "Is it my turn to entertain the master, Mackenzie?"

Mackenzie stood on the dais, arms folded across his chest. "I've already told you, Willie, I need to hear your poem before I'll let you take your turn."

Lillian nudged Fabian's elbow. "I should like to hear the poem. I imagine the hours spent at sea would give a man time for reflection."

Life aboard a ship was far removed from what one read in romantic poems. Food was scarce, illness rife, the weather unpredictable. "We're talking about Willie. Every word he knows rhymes with ale." Fabian cleared his throat. It seems he would grant his wife anything. "Let him recite his poem, Mackenzie."

Mackenzie frowned and shook his head. "Don't say I didn't warn you."

Willie grinned and bowed so low his chin almost touched his knees. "I can't take the credit for the words, my lord, but it is a sediment I share all the same."

"You mean sentiment, Willie."

"That's what I said, my lord, sediment."

Fabian pursed his lips. "Then Lady Ravenscroft is most eager to hear what is in your heart."

Willie nodded and straightened. *"There was an old man who peed in the sea. The sea was too wide, so he peed in the tide, and all the wee fishes crawled up his backside."*

"That's enough of that nonsense," Mackenzie roared, jumping down from the dais to shoo Willie back to his seat. "Have you forgotten there are ladies present? Never mind about the wee fishes. You'll feel my boot up your bahooky if you carry on in that manner."

Lillian chuckled. "I found it rather amusing. At least it rhymed."

"Willie meant no disrespect. A man cannot flout the rules of propriety if he doesn't know they exist." Fabian had lived alongside his men for years. He could tell from the sudden change in the air that they were growing restless. "But I think it's time to send them on their way."

Fabian cleared his throat and raised a brow at Mackenzie who understood his meaning.

Mackenzie strode back to his seat on the dais and banged his gavel on the block. "It's time to bring the celebrations to a close. Now, will you all join me in raising a toast to Lord and Lady Ravenscroft."

Everyone came to their feet and raised their tankards and mugs in salute.

"Perhaps his lordship might like to say a few words about his new bride," Mackenzie said.

Fabian glared. Damn the man. Despite offering many comments to the contrary, Mackenzie knew full well theirs was a marriage of convenience. What the hell was he to say? That he had drugged and kidnapped the lady and bribed her to marry him?

His men's cheers forced him to stand. He turned to face Lillian, not knowing where the devil to start.

Lillian's anxious gaze swept over him. He noticed her nibbling the inside of her cheek as she stroked the gold locket. How could he compete with a lost love? What could he say that would soothe the pain he'd caused?

"It doesn't matter," she whispered as a tense silence permeated the room. "Just raise your glass and sit down."

The hint of hopelessness in her voice roused the chivalrous knight in him. No, he couldn't lie to her. And so all he could do was take her hand, piece together snippets of the truth and hope it conveyed a level of affection.

Her fingers were cold, shaking.

"I've known Lady Ravenscroft for most of my life." Those who had sailed the ship to bring her to Raven Island knew only that they were ferrying his bride. Those trusted men who'd taken her from Vauxhall knew of his real motive. "But I remember the first time I saw her, not as a friend of my sister's or as a neighbour, but someone I admired in her own right."

Lillian squeezed his fingers as she stared up at him.

"Like the stars that guide us on our perilous voyages, she has always been constant, always true and unswerving in her devotion to others." He thought of her love for her brother, of the sacrifices she'd made for him, for Estelle. "And so I ask you to raise a toast to my wife. A woman whose outward beauty gives but a glimpse of the magnificence within."

The women in the audience sighed. The men nudged and winked as they cried, "Lady Ravenscroft!"

Fabian swallowed a mouthful of wine and dropped into his seat.

"Thank you," Lillian whispered. "You didn't have to say such nice things."

He forced himself to look at her, despite knowing that the sight of her watery eyes would be like a knife to his heart.

"I meant every word."

"What we all want is to see you kiss your bride," Freddie shouted.

Lillian inhaled sharply at the brash comment.

"Curb your tongue," Fabian bellowed from his throne seat. Failing to possess an ounce of sophistication or good breeding, his men would goad him until he surrendered. "You must learn to mind your manners when in the company of my wife."

"I mean no disrespect, my lord, but tis a custom."

Fabian raised a brow. "Next you'll tell me it's a custom for the bride to kiss all the men present." The comment received a few chuckles.

Nancy Hill stood. "A kiss in front of witnesses is a token of your troth. A kiss is more than a sign of affection. It's a sharing of souls. Of a promise made."

All eyes fixed on him. The women would doubt his integrity if he did not do as they asked.

Fabian captured Lillian's hand and pressed a kiss on her knuckles. "There, will that not suffice?"

"You've kissed your horse with more passion, my lord."

He cast Lillian a sidelong glance. "Mackenzie's ale has bolstered their courage. They won't settle until we've done the deed."

The calls for them to show some display of affection escalated. Drumming his fingers on the table, Isaac beat out an annoying rhythm, and others soon joined him.

"They mean no harm." Fabian had grown used to their wild ways. "They like to taunt and tease. As their lord and master, I can throw them all out if it pleases you." One growl would send the mischievous pups running for their basket.

Lillian searched his face, her gaze falling to his lips. "Do you think they will accept a kiss on the cheek?"

"I'm afraid not. Sailors are a suspicious lot."

"Then you should kiss me before they raise the roof."

Fabian swallowed. Heaven help him, he felt like a boy fresh from the schoolroom. He bent his head until he was so close her breath breezed across his lips.

He cradled her soft cheeks and touched his lips to hers, a chaste press of the mouth that he expected to last mere seconds. But something happened in that uncomfortable moment. A sudden spark of energy. A shift in the earth's axis. A change of temperature, as if a Divine force sought to bless their union?

Lillian opened her mouth slightly as her hand came to rest on his shoulder. Fabian stilled. Every nerve in his body sprang to life. The urge to devour her, to sate the clawing hunger in his belly came upon him from nowhere.

It was as if no one else in the world existed.

His hand slipped from her cheek to cup her neck as he coaxed her lips apart with the tip of his tongue. Good God, she tasted sweeter than honey. Her soft hum of appreciation sent a rush of blood to his cock. The floral scent of her skin assaulted his senses. Her beguiling essence surrounded him, pulling him deeper into the depths of his desire. He was so damn hard he couldn't think. A fierce need to push into her body took hold. He wanted her in his bed, beneath him, on top of him.

Somewhere in the distance, he heard Mackenzie's voice. "Happen that's our cue to leave."

Fabian ignored the scrape of benches on the flagstones. He ignored the receding footsteps and the bang of the old oak doors. How could he focus on anything else when he'd been snared by a siren?

CHAPTER EIGHT

For the first time in her life, Lillian knew what it was like to kiss a man and mean it. When she'd kissed Lord Martin, she experienced something akin to a weak flutter in her chest. But all expectations fell hopelessly short when compared to kissing Fabian. No amount of daydreaming had prepared her for the wild rush as her blood raced through her veins. Never had she imagined feeling a fire burning hot between her thighs, nor the strange pulsing that suggested she needed something more satisfying.

Intrigued by the flurry of strange sensations, she met Fabian's mouth with equal enthusiasm and swept her tongue against his. A growl rumbled in the back of his throat, and despite angling his head, he couldn't seem to kiss her deeply enough.

Just like the night Mackenzie abducted her from Vauxhall, events happened so quickly she couldn't quite catch her breath. Lips locked together, Fabian drew her to her feet. With one swipe of his arm, he cleared away the cutlery and plates and sent them crashing to the floor. Strong hands fixed on her waist, and he raised her up to sit on the table.

The musky scent clinging to his clothes teased her senses. Her head whirled, but it had nothing to do with drinking potent punch and everything to do with the man running his hand up past the top of her stocking.

Please, Fabian. Don't make me want you.

Sweet heaven. His caress wrung a sigh from somewhere deep in her chest. She had waited a lifetime to feel lust, to feel anything remotely close. She had waited so long to taste the only man ever to visit her in her dreams.

The thought forced her to tear her mouth from his. Wanting Fabian would only cause further pain.

"What's wrong?" Fabian panted. "There's no one here. The men left minutes ago."

She hadn't noticed. Oddly, she didn't care. "It's not supposed to be like this." Experience had taught her to handle rejection. Indifference she could cope with. But this ... the power of it robbed her of all logical thought.

Fabian frowned. "What are you afraid of?"

"Afraid?" She gave a mocking snort. "I'm not afraid, Fabian." She was petrified. What if she grew fond of him? What if she craved his company?

The pads of his fingers stroked circles on her upper thigh. "Don't pretend you don't like it when I touch you."

Lord above. How easy would it be to lie back and take him into her body? Would she feel the same sense of coldness and disgust she'd suffered at Lord Martin's hands? Might she feel differently with Fabian?

"Everything is happening too quickly. Two days ago, I stood watching the balloon at Vauxhall. Now I sit here the wife of a man who admits to using me for his own gain." The truth sliced through her lonely heart. "You expect too much from me."

His hand slipped from her thigh, and she almost cried out in anguish for the loss. But this was lust, not intimacy, she reminded herself.

"I expect nothing and take only the gifts you are willing to bestow." He stepped away and straightened his coat. "We must find a way to muddle through this mess together."

There it was, the one word that promised more than she could give. In the eyes of God, they were joined together, were husband and wife together—so why did she still feel so dreadfully alone?

"Give me a little time."

"Time is something we do not have. You know what will happen when Vane arrives." A frustrated sigh left his lips. "Every day we delay is another day Estelle is out there suffering."

Despite everything she'd said, the need to soothe him took hold. "We don't know that. We must hope that her circumstances are not as dire as you fear."

The change in him was instant. Lillian watched the curtain fall, watched him retreat to his inner sanctum, to the place one escaped to in their mind when reality became too painful to contemplate.

"Come." He offered his hand. "Allow me to give you a tour of the castle. It will serve as a distraction, for both of us."

She spent the next few hours with Fabian, wandering the dark corridors, strolling around the grounds of the castle and meeting all the servants. He took her down to the cove, where they threw pebbles into the water and ambled along the sandy beach while he regaled her with tales of his adventures at sea. Like the man she'd known years ago, he was charming, courteous, shrugged out of his coat and draped it over her shoulders when the wind grew bitter. But whenever the conversation turned to Vane, the cold, cynical pirate surfaced to mock and sneer.

Lillian knew to ignore his snipes. Vane would behave in the same way if she was the one lost at sea. When reunited, perhaps both men would cast aside their differences in a bid to find Estelle. That's if Fabian lived long enough to explain his actions, and if Vane chose to listen.

On their return to the castle, they met Mackenzie. "May I have a wee moment of your time, my lord?" The man struggled to keep the frown from his brow.

Fabian cast her a sidelong glance and waited for her nod of approval before moving to a space a few feet away, a place the men presumed was out of earshot.

Lillian fiddled with the silk ribbon on her dress while she strained to listen to their conversation. From what she could gather, when Fabian's men were transporting the reverend to the mainland, they spotted another small boat on the far side of the island. A hulking figure clambered from the vessel and came ashore.

"Duncan turned around and came straight back." Possessed with such a deep voice, Mackenzie struggled to whisper. "He examined the boat and scoured the cove but found no sign of the stranger."

"Was it Doyle?" Fabian spoke in a low, hushed tone.

"Duncan said not."

"What about Trevane?"

Mackenzie shrugged.

"A treasure hunter?"

"He had no tools."

"Move the boat. Post men at the dock. Whoever he is, leave him no means of escape." Fabian cast her a sidelong glance. His expression darkened. "Keep the gates closed, and the doors locked until we've established who he is and what he wants here."

"Aye, my lord. I'll see to it at once." Mackenzie gave a curt nod and marched away.

Fabian forced a smile as he returned to her side. "Perhaps we should retire for the evening. You may rest in your chamber, but should you leave the room I must insist that you inform me of your whereabouts."

Lillian snorted. "What happened to me wearing breeches and letting my hair blow freely in the wind?"

"It is merely a precaution."

"Why, because you fear Vane has come to take me home?"

The muscle in his jaw flexed as if warming up for a battle. "This is your home now. Vane will have to kill me before I'll let him take you anywhere."

Stunned, Lillian jerked her head back. Her shock had nothing to do with his comment but more her reaction to it. Rather than repel her, the possessiveness in his tone touched her heart. How was that possible? She'd married Fabian hoping to break free from the controlling attitude of society and men. But it wasn't just that. An icy shiver raced through her body as she imagined Fabian collapsing to the ground, blood oozing from a wound to his chest.

"Vane won't kill you." The steely thread of determination in her voice sounded convincing. "He shot Lord Martin for dishonouring me."

"Am I any different?"

If Fabian knew the truth, he would not dare compare himself to that blackguard. "That is hardly a question a man asks his wife on their wedding day. Besides, Vane has no desire to see me in widow's weeds." She sucked in a breath, pained by the thought of losing this irritating man even though he cared nothing for her.

Fabian remained silent although his pursed lips suggested he had more to say on the subject of Vane.

Lillian straightened. "If we are to muddle through this mess, as you suggested, we cannot keep secrets." Heavens above, was she not the worst kind of hypocrite? "You spoke of another man, Doyle. Do you fear he is the one who arrived by boat?"

"Let us be clear about one thing. I fear no man—not Vane, and certainly not Doyle." His gaze swept over her. "But Doyle is unpredictable. He uses underhanded techniques to make his point. Hence, my concern for your safety and that of my men."

"You needn't worry about me." The annoying butterfly in her stomach fluttered about again, seeming to like it when he made a fuss. "If you give me what I asked for then I am more than capable of protecting myself."

"You speak of a sword and pistols?" Amusement flashed in his eyes. "What if Doyle drugs your drink and lures you away under false pretences? What will you do then?"

She shrugged. "Whatever it takes to escape. Consequently, I have another request to make. I want a blade and sheath. Something small, easily concealed, perhaps with a strap and buckle."

Fabian arched a brow. "You certainly know how to pique a man's interest." His gaze dropped to her bodice and then meandered all the way down to her toes. "For now, I shall grant your request. But at some point in the future, when you feel able, you will tell me what happened to you."

Panic flared. "I don't know what you mean."

He closed the gap between them and his dark eyes fixed firmly on her. "Oh, you do. A lady does not demand weapons unless she fears for her life. You know *I* would never hurt you. But someone has."

The conversation brought painful memories flooding back. Things that had no place in her mind on such a special day as this. "Let's just say"—she stopped abruptly and swallowed to lubricate her dry throat—"you're not the only man who has used me to hurt Vane."

The blood drained from his face, leaving him deathly pale. "The difference is I shall spend the rest of my life making amends. I intend to ensure you find happiness here."

If only he'd added *with me.*

A chill shivered through her, but she pushed his coat off her shoulders and handed the garment back to him. "Let's go inside. There must be plenty of weapons here. A man doesn't sail the seas without an armoury." The chest of swords on the ship told her as much. "Should Doyle attempt anything foolish, it would help to know what he looks like and what his motive is for wanting to cause you harm."

Fabian shrugged into his coat. The material bulged around the muscles in his arms, and her traitorous fingers itched to explore the contours. "Doyle is a large man with jowls rather than a jawline and hands the size of mallets."

"Does he by any chance have access to a black carriage and have cheeks pitted with scars?" Since arriving at the castle, she'd not seen the pock-faced man. One did not forget a face like that, particularly not one sporting a menacing grin.

Fabian frowned. "No, but Doyle may have a scar above his right eye where I punched him so hard it split the skin."

"So Doyle is not the pock-faced man?"

"A few men here suffer from skin conditions. It's a common complaint when one spends so much time at sea. None of them accompanied Mackenzie to London." He paused. "Perhaps the effects of the laudanum played tricks with your memory. Did you notice someone at Vauxhall with a similar affliction?"

Her fractured memories were impossible to piece together. But she'd seen the man days before her excursion to the Pleasure Gardens. "The man with the scars sat atop an unmarked carriage. I watched him circle Berkeley Square. I looked directly into his cold eyes when he stopped outside my window." She shook her head and muttered to herself as she revisited the scene. "But when I asked Mackenzie, he confirmed *he* was the one who stopped outside my window."

Perhaps sensing her disquiet, Fabian captured her hand. "I'll speak to Mackenzie, but he assures me they met with no one in London. Perhaps it has nothing to do with you, and someone is interested in monitoring your brother's movements."

Logically that made sense. "You might be right." Ladies often boasted of an affair with Vane to make their husbands jealous. Still, the heavy weight in her chest and the ache in her throat suggested otherwise.

Fabian placed her hand in the crook of his arm and led her inside. "Doyle worked on *The Octavia*."

"The ship captained by Mr Hill?"

"Yes." He seemed surprised she knew. "One of my competitors paid Doyle to spoil the cargo. I think he hoped to ruin my reputation so other merchants thought twice about hiring us to transport their goods."

"A ruined reputation can wreak untold damage." She knew that better than most.

"The fool almost sank the ship and killed us all."

"No wonder you punched him." They passed the door leading to the great hall, and she suddenly remembered her flowers. "Would you mind if I collect my posy? I left it on the table during the feast." If she hoped to preserve the pretty heads she needed to press them before they wilted.

"Not at all."

Lillian hurried into the great hall expecting the room to be as they had left it. But the place was cold now, quiet, the tables empty, the floor clear of any debris. Those few hours spent in celebration were amongst the happiest of her life. How strange she should feel that way? Sentiment had no place in what was essentially a business contract. Still, she liked Fabian—she always had.

She found her flowers on the long table, sitting in a tankard of water, and so shook away the droplets clinging to the stems. Her gaze drifted to the throne chairs, to the place she'd first kissed her husband. A chuckle escaped her lips when she thought of all the times she'd dreamed of kissing Fabian Darcy. Of course, she'd imagined sweet nips and chaste pecks, not the hot sinful way he'd devoured her mouth.

It seemed the man did everything with mastery and skill. Was that part of his appeal? A vision of his muscular arms and well-defined chest flashed into her mind. Would he approach their lovemaking in the same way? She snorted. Lovemaking? Just like her experience with Lord Martin, love played no part.

Her stomach roiled when the memory of her ruination flooded her mind. How had she been so foolish? How had she been so blind?

Darkness descended like a black choking fog. In an instant, she saw Lord Martin's kind face, saw the mask slip to reveal the monster hidden beneath. Never had she met a man so cold, so heartless. One so skilled in the art of deception.

"What's the delay?" Fabian's rich voice drifted over her, banishing her nightmare. "If you're looking for wine to bolster your courage I can have a bottle sent to your chamber?"

She clutched the posy, pasted a smile and swung around to face him. "And pray tell me why I would need courage?"

Fabian folded his arms across his chest and gave a devilish grin. "Is this not our wedding day? Are there not certain matters that require our attention?"

He held the same boyish charm she'd seen in their youth, and Lillian drank in the sight like a woman parched.

A nervous flutter in her throat forced her to swallow. "While I'm obliged to do my duty—"

"Duty?" he mocked. "Trust me, love, it will be no hardship."

Her cheeks flushed hotly under the heat of his stare. But, despite the vow she'd made, she was not ready to bare herself body and soul. "Men think differently about such matters. You must give me more time."

Fabian stepped back and gestured to the corridor. "Let us continue this discussion upstairs. There's something I want to give you." His eyes sparkled with mischief. Never had she seen a more handsome man. "Don't look so frightened. I have a wedding present for you ... something that should sit nicely in your warm palm."

Lillian arched a brow.

"Have no fear, I shall keep my clothes on when I give it to you." He pushed his hand through his mop of ebony hair. "Why is it that whatever I say sounds highly inappropriate?"

She laughed then. "I think it has something to do with your husky tone."

"Can I help it if I find the prospect of bedding my wife appealing?"

How her shaking limbs supported her weight, she'd never know. "Come," she said as she walked past him and out into the corridor, "I'm keen to see my gift."

"Let's hope it's not too thick for your dainty fingers to grasp."

Oh, the man was incorrigible.

Once upstairs, he entered his chamber. Lillian hovered outside.

"You can come in." Fabian sounded highly amused. "And I suggest you close the door. We wouldn't want anyone to catch us in the act."

"Know that your efforts to tease me are in vain." She stepped into the inherently masculine space.

Rich oak panels lined the walls of his bedchamber. Curtains of forest-green velvet hung from the poster bed. The room reflected the dark, sensual character of its master. The pile of books on the side table spoke of the younger man who believed knowledge was power, the key to all of life's conundrums.

He strode to the bed, and with his back to her fiddled with a wooden box. Lillian took a moment to close her eyes and inhale the aroma. Fabian's essence permeated the room. It was a different smell than she remembered. Notes of frankincense and sandalwood mingled with the fresh salty scent of the sea. The natural yet exotic fragrance spoke of maturity and mystery as opposed to youth.

"Keep your eyes closed and hold out your hand," he said. "See how it feels when you wrap your fingers around this beauty."

She obliged him, gasped at the sudden weight in her palm.

Fabian's hand supported hers. "Is it not smooth and hard at the same time?"

"You speak of the wood." Lillian opened her eyes and glanced at the pistol.

"It's French but should serve you well while I arrange for a replacement."

Lillian examined the barrel, hammer and frisson. She squeezed her right eye shut and aimed at the window.

"You have a steady hand." Fabian stepped aside. "I trust you know how to load and fire the weapon?"

"Of course." She offered a confident grin. "My brother never shirks his responsibilities."

"That remains to be seen."

She ignored his quip. Until he had a frank conversation with Vane, he would always believe his own version of events. "Is the pistol one of a pair?"

"I'm afraid not."

"May I see the box?"

"Certainly." He gestured to the bed. "Sit down if you wish. As you'll be sleeping with me tonight, I suggest you make yourself comfortable."

Lillian tutted. Why would she sleep with him when she had her own chamber? "Must we go over this again?"

He stepped closer and placed his hand on her upper arm. "A stranger has come ashore. Lord knows how many men seek satisfaction for your brother's misdeeds. Lord knows, there are plenty of men keen to see me fail, too."

"One thing is certain. If Vane were here, he'd be hammering the gates demanding entrance."

Fabian sighed. "I agree. If it's Doyle, I suspect he'll cling to the walls like a limpet hoping to remain undetected." He glanced at the large bed. "You'll sleep here tonight, where I know you're safe."

Something in his tone suggested she should heed his words. "You say sleep but are you certain that's what you mean?"

He caressed her upper arm, the gesture more protective than a prelude to seduction. "You may wear your nightgown and bring your pistol, though I'd rather not wake in the night to feel something hard and solid pressing into my back."

She didn't have a nightgown, only her chemise. "A wall of pillows will prevent any misunderstanding. We shall keep to our own side."

Fabian's hand slipped from her arm. "Are we to sleep like enemies, too? Are we to remain on opposite ends of the battlefield with our defences raised?"

"For the time being."

He shook his head. "Then allow me to give you some space to grow accustomed to your surroundings. If you have no objection, I shall accompany Mackenzie on a tour of the area. All I ask is that you stay in this room until I return."

"Of course. Only a lady promised freedom might think she had the right to wander."

"You shall have your freedom, my lady. Ask anyone here. The Raven never goes back on his word." With that, Fabian inclined his head. "Will you wait up for me?"

"Do I have a choice? Or are you inclined to make more demands?"

A mischievous grin formed on his lips. "Were I so inclined, I'd seek more than just your company."

She wanted to offer a witty retort, but the heated look in his eyes stole her breath. "I can't promise I won't fall asleep."

"I can't promise I won't try to wake you."

They stared at each other, neither blinked. It became a battle of wills as to who would look away first. With his eyes still fixed on her, he stepped forward. Lillian swallowed. He bent his head until he was so close their breath mingled in the air between them. "Will you miss me when I'm gone?"

Good Lord, the man *was* a pirate, with an ability to avoid detection and steal away her soul. To protect her poor battered heart, she had no choice but to sever the connection.

"Mackenzie must be waiting," she said, stepping back.

"Then I shall bid you good night—for now."

"Good night, Fabian." She turned away and strode over to the window. When the door clicked shut, she wrapped her arms across her chest and released a weary sigh. Being in his company proved tiring as she struggled to fight the obsession she'd held for as long as she could remember.

She opened the arched window that gave a perfect view of the landscape and inhaled the fresh sea air. She must have waited ten minutes before she saw Fabian ride out with Mackenzie at his side. They galloped across the heathland, out of view. A sudden frisson of fear made her shudder. Vane was not a man who skulked in the shadows. Had her brother been aboard the rowboat he would have raced to the castle gates in his hunt to find and punish Fabian.

So that left Doyle. But why would a traitor return to the fold knowing he would receive a hostile reception? What motive could he possibly have other than a desire for vengeance?

CHAPTER NINE

It was dark when Fabian and Mackenzie returned to the castle. The cold light of the moon illuminated their way. As did the amber flames in the braziers scattered around the bailey. The weather had hindered their search, the relentless downpour lasting for more than an hour. Fat droplets of rain had pelted their cheeks and clung to their lashes making it impossible to see anything more than a few feet ahead.

"Lord, can you credit our luck?" Mackenzie dismounted and thrust his hand through hair more frizzy now than straight. "Only when we return home do the clouds depart to destinations new."

Fabian swung down to the ground. "Well, at least we know the blackguard's not hiding in the cottages."

"Aye, I suppose we should count our blessings as it gave me an opportunity to question Mary."

"Did you mention the missing food?"

"Och, the woman's terrified to leave the house for fear someone will blame her for what happened with Doyle."

"And he's not stolen ashore to visit her since we cast him out?"

"She says not, and I believe her. I cannot help but feel sorry for the woman." That came as no surprise. Mackenzie felt sorry for everyone. "From where I stand we've two choices. We can suggest she goes to stay with her sister in Truro."

Mary had been a part of their community for years. It felt wrong to punish her for her husband's failings. "And the other option?"

"We help her to regain everyone's trust. We could bring her to the castle. Let her serve as maid to Lady Ravenscroft."

Fabian considered his friend's eagerness to help. While Mackenzie's heart melted whenever he heard a sad story, did his desire to assist Mary stem from more than a need to be kind? "Did you say you knew Mary before she married Doyle?"

A flush crept up the man's cheeks. Even his ears turned red. "Aye, when she lived in Truro. Her father owned an inn, and she often served food and cleaned tables."

"And you did not think to court the woman yourself?"

Mackenzie averted his gaze. "Well, I ... she's a good ten years younger. It's not so much of a problem now as it was back then."

"I am almost six years older than Lady Ravenscroft." Then again, the way he looked at Lillian now differed vastly from the way he'd looked at her as a girl. The thought drew his gaze up to his bedchamber window. The soft glow of candlelight radiated out into the darkness, and he wondered if his wife awaited him in bed.

"Happen it's of no consequence."

"Why? Doyle might well be dead." When a man turned traitor, he invariably had enemies on both sides. Everyone distrusted a turncoat, even those who offered the bribe. "For all we know, Mary could be a widow."

Something akin to hope flashed in Mackenzie's eyes, and Fabian cursed himself for not noticing his friend's attachment before.

"I'll speak to Lady Ravenscroft. She might agree to take Mary as her maid." It was only right he support Mackenzie's altruistic efforts. But it was not his place to choose his wife's attendants.

Mackenzie inclined his head and then gathered Thunder's reins. "I'll take the horses to the stable. No doubt you want out of those wet clothes. And it's your wedding night. Happen there's a warmer place you'd rather be."

The thought of drawing Lillian's body close and feeling her soft skin against his, sent his blood rushing through his veins. Of course, he'd need strength and skill in the art of seduction if he hoped to break down her barricade.

"Then I shall bid you a good night." The sudden urge to slip into bed next to his wife took hold. "Keep me informed should those on watch notice anything suspicious."

They parted ways.

Despite the weight of his sodden clothes, Fabian mounted the stone steps with speed and agility. And yet that was not the cause of his racing heart. Reaching his chamber door, he lingered outside for a moment. If he could just stop his thoughts jumping forward to the moment he settled between Lillian's silky thighs he might survive the next few minutes without spilling himself in his breeches.

He turned the handle, half expecting to find the door locked. The fact it was open proved promising.

Fabian slipped inside and eased the door closed. Wood crackled in the stone hearth, the orange glow of the fire setting a scene ripe for seduction. His gaze fell to the woman sleeping in his bed, her ebony hair draped across her shoulder, her delicate fingers clutching the pillow she used as a barrier to keep him out.

Rooted to the spot, he listened to her gentle breath breezing through the room. Each exhalation did odd things to the hairs on his nape. Each peaceful sigh sent his thoughts scattering in opposing directions. This lady had the power to rouse chivalry in his chest and lust in his loins.

As a gentleman, he'd be damned before he'd take a woman who didn't want him. And so he crept over to the fire and stripped naked in the hope the heat from the flames would warm his clammy skin.

A slight hitch in her breath forced him to glance back over his shoulder, but she had not moved and still held the same angelic look he'd witnessed moments earlier. When his muscles no longer felt numb, he washed the spots of mud from his face. The longer he stood there, bare as the day he was born, the more amorous thoughts filled his head.

As a distraction, he found his telescope and stared out of the window. He could see the sea stretching as far as the horizon, the light from the moon casting a silvery path across the surface. He could see the heathland surrounding the castle's high walls, the carpet of purple heather and wild yellow flowers less vibrant now. A sudden movement in the shadows drew his gaze but with neither man nor beast visible he suspected a nocturnal creature.

Placing his telescope on the stone sill, he turned to the bed. Lillian looked so beautiful and serene the sight rendered him frozen to the spot. Devil take him. Why could he not simply climb in next to her? He'd sailed through winds strong enough to uproot trees, felt the boom of thunder shake him to his core. Surely he could lay next to a woman and do nothing but sleep.

But this wasn't just any woman.

Feeling like a boy on the first day of boarding school, he peeled back the coverlet and slipped beneath the cool sheets. One plump pillow separated them. But the bag of feathers might just as well be a stone wall.

Before closing his eyes, he took one last look at Lillian. They were joined as man and wife, bound together in the eyes of God. Somehow he had to find a way to break down her barrier. Somehow he had to make her want him.

Lillian heard Fabian return from his search for the stranger. How could she sleep when his safety had suddenly become her priority? She'd exerted every effort to keep her breathing slow and shallow. Another awkward conversation about marriage and duty would not solve the problem. Intimacy was not something one forced. Still, catching sight of his firm buttocks as he warmed himself in front of the fire, awakened a desperate desire to be close to him.

So why was she clinging to the pillow as if she were alone in a rough sea and it was the only thing keeping her afloat?

An hour passed.

The fire in the hearth no longer burned with the same intensity. The man at her side slept peacefully. Indeed, she could not tear her gaze away from the soft rise and fall of his bare chest. The urge to run her fingers over the dusting of dark hair, over the sculpted planes of his abdomen, took hold. So why were her limbs frozen, incapable of acting no matter how tempting the thought?

Knowing sleep would elude her until she found a way to calm her thoughts, she slipped out of bed. For fear of waking Fabian, she padded over to the fire and stood there warming her hands. The glow gave off enough light to read, though all the books stacked on the side table related to philosophy. After her dreadful experiences, she did not need an education in the principles of behaviour. Besides, she had Fabian to challenge her viewpoint now.

"Come back to bed, Lillian." Fabian's voice was deeper and raspier than usual. The sound stroked her senses. The man made it impossible for her to fight her attraction.

"I'm not tired." It took her a moment to rouse the courage to turn around. The sight of him sitting up on his elbows, of his mussed hair and bristly jaw stole her breath. "I thought I might read." She gestured to one of two chairs flanking the fire.

"Do you desire company?"

Oh, why had he used that word? Since marrying Fabian she suddenly desired a great many things. An image of thick thighs and bare buttocks flashed into her mind. "No. You need sleep."

"Sleep is not my main priority." His gaze drifted over the front of her chemise. "You do know that garment is practically sheer. In the light of the fire, I can see the outline of every curve." A hum left his lips. "I can see—"

"Yes, yes. Perhaps it's not the best choice, but I have nothing else to wear to bed." Her cheeks burned, and she moved to the window. Each step seemed clumsy and awkward under the weight of his stare.

"Oh, I'm not complaining."

She picked up the telescope and gazed out at the sea. Well, she pretended to look, but the naked man in the bed behind her dominated her thoughts.

"How do you find the view?"

"Breathtaking."

"I agree." He sighed. "It's rather spectacular from this angle, too. When you lean forward the material clings to every place a husband can dare to look."

Lillian tried to swallow past the lump in her throat. She daren't move. All she could do was grip the brass object, stare out into the night and wait for her heart to stop hammering in her ears.

She followed the moon's reflection on the water, all the time aware of Fabian's gaze caressing her back. "After such a terrible storm, the night is calm and peaceful." Unlike the whirlwind of emotions wreaking havoc with her body. "There's enough light to see quite far into the distance."

"If you look west you can see the church. If you're struggling to find it, I can offer my assistance."

She brought her focus back to the castle wall, hoping to trace the path along the coastline to the small stone building where she had pledged her troth. Her gaze drifted past the tall shadow mistaking it for a tree. But there were no trees on the heathland. Holding the scope close to her eye, she skimmed back to the strange grey outline.

"Have you found it?"

"I've found something." The shadow stopped moving, and she realised it was a man. The moon cast an eerie sheen over the figure's face. Lillian's heart dropped like a lead weight into her stomach. "There's a man outside." Something about him seemed familiar. It wasn't Vane. This man had a bulky frame, fat as opposed to solid muscle.

"Did you say a man?"

The figure raised his chin and looked up at the castle giving a better view of his face. Lillian blinked rapidly. The telescope slipped from her hand. She gasped, her throat so tight she could barely breathe. "It—it's the pock-faced man." The words were a strangled cry.

Fabian threw the coverlet back and jumped out of bed. Undeterred by his nakedness he strode over to the window, picked up the telescope and looked out at the monster who'd haunted her dreams for weeks.

"What the blazes?"

Lillian stood a mere inch from hard muscles and bronzed skin, and tried to regain her composure. All thoughts should have been on the beastly figure outside who had somehow followed her to Raven Island. But how could she think of anything but the impressive gentleman at her side? She watched him, mesmerised by the bulging biceps in his arms. Try as she might, she couldn't prevent her gaze dropping to his narrow hips, lower still.

"It's hard to see clearly from this angle," he complained.

"Indeed." Her word was more a purr.

"You're certain it's the man who frightened you in London?"

"I'm certain. I shall never forget the evil look in his eye."

Fabian handed her the telescope and turned to face her. "Stay here."

Dwarfed by the expanse of his bare chest, she gulped. "Why, what do you intend to do?"

"The only way to find out what he's doing here is to ask him."

Fear gripped her. "Surely you don't mean to go out there?" She touched his arm and their eyes locked.

"Why else is he here if not for you? I want to know how he knew where to come and why. I made an oath. I promised you freedom, not a life where you're confined to your room and under constant threat."

She glanced at the window, looking for the source of the sudden chill in the air. "Fabian, he does not seem like the sort of man who likes talking. What if he hurts you?"

A smile touched the corners of his lips. He bent his head and brushed a chaste kiss over her mouth. "He won't. Regardless of what happens, you're to stay here."

He did not give her a chance to reply. In less than a minute, he'd thrown on breeches, boots and a shirt. She hadn't realised that watching a man dress could be so enthralling.

"Lock the door," was all he said as he darted from the room.

Lillian paced the floor. Fabian had left without a sword or pistol. What use were fists if the beast had a weapon? She would call Mackenzie if only she knew which room was his.

Knots formed in her stomach. The Lord saw fit to punish her at every turn. Was she to lose her husband, too? She clutched the locket at her throat. Many times she'd been powerless to prevent Fate's cruel hands. But she was tired of being weak and vulnerable.

With steely determination, she strode through the connecting door and into her chamber. She found the mahogany box, removed and loaded the pistol. With no time to dress she returned to Fabian's room, pushed her feet into her slippers, grabbed his damp coat from the floor and shrugged into the garment.

The corridors were empty. No one stood guard at the gate. Relief flooded her chest. Surely Fabian's man had accompanied him in his pursuit of the stranger. Lillian slipped out into the night, realising her mistake as soon as she crossed the heathland and spiky sprigs of heather stabbed her toes. Silk slippers were no match for sturdy boots when it came to midnight hikes.

Still, she fought on, eager to find Fabian.

Gruff shouts reached her ears. Squinting in the darkness, she noticed two black figures in the distance. Only when they merged into one did she realise they were wrestling. Lillian cocked her pistol and crept closer.

"You'll tell me what I want to know, damn it." Fabian punched the man hard on the jaw. The beast stumbled back but kept his footing and followed with a right-handed jab Fabian was agile enough to dodge. "What is she to you?"

Bouncing lightly on the balls of his feet, Fabian dealt the man a blow to the stomach. The figure groaned but lunged forward. He grabbed Fabian around the waist and tackled him to the ground.

Lillian thought to take aim as a warning, but she had one shot and knew to use it wisely.

The men rolled around amidst the low growing vegetation. Punches flew. Despite numerous grunts and groans, it was impossible to tell who had the upper hand. If this were a boxing match, she'd put her money on Fabian. But based on brute strength, the pockmarked man was a force to be reckoned.

"Go near her again and I'll kill you." Fabian's threat hung in the air. He pushed the rogue onto his back and struck him hard on the nose. A sharp cracked accompanied the spurt of blood and an agonising howl.

"Not if I kill you first."

A flash of light caught Lillian's eye. Only when the rogue raised his hand did she notice he'd drawn a blade. With no time to think, she aimed and fired. The ball flew through the air at lightning speed, hit the metal tip and sent the knife flying out of the man's hand.

"What the—? You almost blew my damn fingers off."

"Trust me. Had that been my intention I would not have missed the target." Arrogance infused her tone. "I could put a ball between your eyes from a hundred yards."

Fabian's head swung around in her direction. "Lillian?"

Having fired her only shot, she had but one option open. She stepped forward, thrust the pistol inside her coat and pretended to pull another. No doubt the beast was too stupid to notice. She aimed it at the man's head. "Would you care to put me to the test?"

The man raised his hands. "Don't shoot. I'm just the hired help. I'll tell you what you want to know."

Fabian stood and scoured the ground for the blade, finding it amid the heather.

The beast scrambled to his feet. The deep indentations in his skin made him appear all the more dark and menacing.

"What are you doing here?" Lillian stared at him over the barrel of her pistol. "You've been following me around London. Why?"

Fabian came to stand at her side. He had a cut across his cheekbone, blood on his lip. For the tenth time in as many hours, her heart softened at the sight of him.

"Who hired you?" Fabian demanded. "Was it Doyle?"

The beast shrugged. "I'm paid to follow Trevane and his sister. I'm to report on their whereabouts."

Lillian took a step forward. "Report to whom?" Lord Martin was dead. After all this time, did his accomplice still bear a grudge? Was it his sole intention to cause mischief?

The beast pursed his lips. "That I cannot say."

"Cannot or will not?" Fabian challenged. "Do you fear this man?"

"I ain't afraid of no one, save perhaps a woman with a pistol."

"What about a Scot with a fiery temper?" Mackenzie marched to their side and thrust his hands on his hips. "Did you not know pickled bollocks are a Highland delicacy?" He turned to Lillian. "Beg your pardon, my lady, for my foul tongue."

"You're forgiven, Mackenzie."

"I won't get paid if I don't report back," the beast complained.

"I'd be more concerned about being hit between the eyes with a lead ball." Lillian cocked the pistol. "Now, give me the name of the person who hired you."

Fabian cleared his throat. "My wife is prone to sudden bouts of anger. I should do what she says else I can guarantee it won't be pretty."

"Your wife?" The news threw the beast off kilter. He shuffled from one foot to the other and held his rough hands up in surrender. "All right. I'll tell you. It was Lord Cornell. He's the one who hired me."

"Cornell?" Lillian could not contain her surprise. The lord had never expressed a grievance. She lowered the pistol. Was Cornell the gentleman who paid Lord Martin to ruin her? Despite Vane's effort to learn the truth, he had failed to uncover a name.

"His lordship hired me when he heard you were back from Italy."

Fabian stepped closer. "And how did you know to come here?"

"I knew the Scot was following the lady." He gestured to Mackenzie, who appeared affronted that anyone would have the nerve to pry into his business. "I tracked them back to the Eight Bells. The landlord said he knew nothing, but his doxy had heard talk of the Raven. When Trevane left Vauxhall without his sister, I knew you'd made your move."

"That does not explain how you found the island." Fabian balled his fists at his sides. Lillian supposed one could not offer a lady freedom if every rogue in London knew where she lived.

"I trailed you along the coast as far as Branscombe. Most people know the Scot. Most people know he lives on the island."

Mackenzie's cheeks ballooned. Lillian didn't know whether he was ashamed or offended. Even so, she didn't care how the blackguard had found them.

"Tell me what Cornell wants." She stepped forward and aimed at the permanent furrows between the man's brows. "Does this have anything to do with Lord Martin?"

Fabian inhaled sharply but said nothing.

The beast raised his hands. "All I know is his lordship won't rest until he's hurt your brother."

"What do you know of Lord Martin?" Lillian gritted her teeth. "Tell me." She was somewhat thankful the barrel of the pistol was empty. Whenever she thought of Lord Martin her head filled with a cloudy haze that obliterated all rational thought.

"His lordship mentioned him." The rogue grimaced. "He said Lord Martin had done his job and now it was up to me to do mine."

The words echoed in Lillian's ears—goading her, taunting her like the spiteful gossips of the *ton*.

She pulled the trigger.

In her mind, she saw the deceitful Lord Martin crumple to the ground in a bloody heap.

Fabian gasped.

The rogue fell back in shock. The acrid scent of urine caught her nose, and she realised the terrifying man with the pockmarked face had piddled in his trousers.

"Make no mistake," she said in a deadly tone, "the next time you cross me I shall blow a hole in your chest. One so large everyone will see you have no heart."

A heavy silence filled the air.

Lillian lowered the pistol, turned on her heels and strode back to the castle alone.

CHAPTER TEN

"So, what shall we do with this sneaky scrote, my lord?" Mackenzie squared his shoulders and snarled at the thug hired to track down Lillian.

With a heavy heart, Fabian dragged his gaze away from the dejected figure of his wife in the distance. Perhaps he should chase after her, but gut instinct told him to give her some time alone before broaching the subject of Lord Martin. Clearly, the gossip making the rounds of the London ballrooms failed to convey the full measure of the story.

"Throw him in the dungeon for the time being." Until in possession of all the facts, Fabian would be foolish to release the man. "He is to stay there until I decide what to do with him."

The blackguard scrambled to his feet. "You've no right to keep me here."

"Och, stop blathering like a bairn. You should save your breath to cool your porridge. That is if we remember to feed you."

"You will come with us quietly, or we'll drag you to the castle."

Mackenzie nodded to the man's trousers and scrunched his

nose. "If you're a good wee laddie I might lend you a clean pair of breeches."

"Breeches?" the rogue scoffed. "I hear you Highlanders wear dresses."

"Enough!" Fabian had no patience for their petty quarrels, not when he had more pressing matters on his mind. "What's your name?"

The rogue hesitated. "What does it matter?"

"Your name," Fabian repeated.

"It's ... it's Aubrey."

"Aubrey?" Mackenzie snorted. "And you have the nerve to tease me for wearing dresses."

While Mackenzie continued baiting the prisoner, Isaac and Freddie came bounding towards them.

"Lady Ravenscroft said you might need help, my lord." Freddie scanned the stranger, one corner of his mouth curling up in disdain. "Is this the crook who came ashore?"

Fabian nodded. "Take him to the dungeon. I'm afraid he's not ready to leave us just yet."

Aubrey craned his neck and gazed across the landscape. He could run, but Fabian would catch him before he'd taken two steps. Being outnumbered, Aubrey had no option but to follow them back to the castle.

Descending the steps into the dungeon, Fabian led the prisoner through the dank underground chamber to the row of cramped cells.

"You can't leave me in here." Aubrey gripped the iron railings and peered into the dark room beyond. "What's that godawful smell?"

Mackenzie sniggered. "I think you'll find that's your trousers."

"Mackenzie will arrange for a brazier and firewood, candles

and bedding." Fabian unlocked the door and gestured for the man to step inside.

A chorus of shrill squeaks accompanied the scratching on the cobblestones. Aubrey swung around. "You expect me to sleep with the rats?"

"It's a temporary measure. Mackenzie will ensure you're as comfortable as possible. Under the circumstances, you should count your blessings. I am within my rights to shoot trespassers."

"Aye, if you're good I might find you a chamber pot, save you piddling in your trousers."

Aubrey growled, but Mackenzie shoved him into the cell and closed the door.

"Can I leave you to deal with Aubrey?" Fabian said, eager to return to his chamber and discuss the matter with his wife.

"Aye, I might fetch Willie and have him recite his poetry. As torture goes, that's worse than spending a few hours on the rack."

Fabian stepped closer to Mackenzie and lowered his voice. "I trust you to take care of the key and ensure the man is fed and watered."

"You needn't worry on that score, my lord."

Fabian inclined his head. "Then I shall leave you here while I attend to Lady Ravenscroft." He turned on his heels and marched back to the narrow flight of stairs leading up to the bailey.

As Fabian raced back through the castle to his chamber, he recalled what he knew of Lillian's scandalous past. The gossip weaving its way through the ballrooms was that Lillian had given herself to her betrothed before having the sense to exchange vows. Lord Martin found the lady to be far too free with her passions and consequently broke the engagement. Fearing her brother's wrath, Martin fled to Italy. Vane caught him and challenged him to a duel. The ladies paid homage to Vane's heroic actions. The gentlemen blamed Lillian's loose morals when the poor lord died.

So what the blazes did Lord Cornell have to do with it all?

Fabian stopped outside his bedchamber door in an effort to calm his breathing. If he hoped to help Lillian, he had to hear the truth. Whatever had happened in the past, clearly Cornell still held a grudge.

Fabian slipped into the room as he'd done hours before when he found Lillian sleeping in his bed. But the bed was empty. His head shot to the chairs flanking the fire, but they were empty, too.

Where the devil was she?

A sigh left his lips. With the intruder caught, she had no need to sleep in his bedchamber. Fabian strode over to the door joining their rooms. It creaked open, the sound loud enough to alert the whole castle of his movements let alone the shadowy figure sitting hunched on the edge of the bed.

"Lillian?"

The icy chill in the air sent a shiver from his shoulders to his toes. The room was dark, except for the patchwork of silver shapes on the floor where slivers of moonlight streamed through the leaded window.

"Lillian?"

She failed to answer.

"Lilly?" It was a name he'd used before. The name of the sweet girl he remembered. The name of the girl untroubled by etiquette and gossip, the one who thought life was an adventure.

She raised her head. "No one calls me Lilly, not even Vane." Her croaky voice caught in her throat.

"I recall you used to like it."

"Say it again."

"Come, Lilly, it's too cold in here." Fabian moved closer. She was still wearing his coat. He reached for her hands and pulled her to her feet. "Come and sit by the fire."

When he met her gaze, the sight sent a stabbing pain right through his heart. Her eyes were sunken and rimmed with brown shadows, the whites littered with red veins. Blotchy cheeks confirmed she'd shed many tears, yet the cause of her torment still lingered in the hazel pools.

"Forgive me." The words tumbled out of his mouth. Guilt surfaced like an angry Poseidon, trident in hand ready to prod him for his misdeeds. Fabian gripped her hands tightly. "Forgive me for behaving like a selfish scoundrel. I should not have brought you here. I should have left you in peace."

"Peace?" Water filled her eyes. A single drop trickled down her nose. "Is there such a thing?"

Feeling an urgent need to soothe her, he cradled her cheeks. "If there is, I'm yet to find it. But I shall not stop looking until I do."

A weak smile formed. "Perhaps we could search *together*."

He bent his head and pressed his lips to hers. The taste of her fed the obsession he'd been harbouring ever since her arrival—for years before that. He broke contact. "I want you to tell me everything."

She swallowed deeply. "Don't ask me to relive the memory. I wake each morning with a desperate need to remember some things, dreading the thought of remembering others."

During the years since Estelle's supposed death, he'd experienced a similar feeling, wanting to remember, wanting to forget. "Emotional pain is like a festering wound. One ignores it at their peril. Tell me what you want me to do, and I shall do it."

"Vane said that, too, just before you abducted me from Vauxhall."

The comment poked at his conscience. "Then I shall take you back to Vane. Focus my efforts on finding Estelle without him, as I should have done in the beginning." The thought of losing Lillian robbed him of breath.

"You don't want me to stay?" A tear fell, the droplet hitting her cheek.

"Of course I want you to stay." He gripped her shoulders. "But I was wrong to play on your weaknesses, wrong to leave you with limited options."

"I want to stay." She swallowed a whimper. "You're my husband. I have nothing else. If I cannot make this work what hope is there?"

The words were sweet music to his ears. "Then allow me to be your husband. Confide in me. Tell me your deepest desires, your darkest secrets. Know I shall not judge you as others are wont to do."

She put a trembling hand to his cheek. The intimacy of the moment touched his soul. "You must help me, Fabian. I do not know who I am. I stare at the looking glass and hardly recognise myself."

"You're Lilly." He forced a grin. "You're the woman who wants to live, not wallow in sorrow."

She blinked, and her eyes brightened. "Then you must remind me of it often." She paused, her gaze dipping to the opening of his shirt. "Let us return to your room. It's too cold in here, and I'm numb to my bones." She took his hand and led him through the connecting door.

"I'll add more wood to the fire." He moved to walk away.

"Wait. I want to tell you what happened." She touched the locket at her throat. "I need to talk to someone. Whenever I broach the subject with Vane guilt eats away at him, and I cannot bear to see him in pain."

"Then sit. I shall pour us a brandy while you warm yourself."

"In a moment." She bit down on her bottom lip, her gaze flitting back and forth, as erratic as her decisions. "There is another matter that requires our attention first."

She shrugged out of his coat and it fell to the floor. In the muted light, he could see the voluptuous curve of her hips through the thin chemise. Pert nipples pressed against the fine material.

She gathered her ebony hair and pulled it over one shoulder. A man would need to be blind not to recognise the signs.

"Are you suggesting we consummate our alliance?"

"It is our wedding night. I … I am not promising it will be a satisfying experience. Indeed, I'm certain you're used to bedding women with far more skill."

"Lilly."

"What?"

"You think too much." Hardly believing his luck, he dragged his shirt over his head and dropped the garment onto the floor. "But I suspect it's because you're afraid you might feel something." He took her hand and placed it on his chest. "I am yours to command. Yours to own."

"But I don't know what to do."

It crossed his mind to ask about her experiences with Lord Martin but thought it unwise to drag her out of this amorous mood. "There are no rules. Follow your heart."

She pursed her lips.

"Whatever you do to me will be pleasurable," he added.

"Am I allowed to explore?" She didn't wait for an answer, but placed both palms on his chest and pushed up to feel the shape of his shoulders. Blood pooled in his cock. Her eyes sparkled with delight when her fingers grazed his nipples and the sensation made him suck in a breath.

"Just like you, certain parts of my body are sensitive to the touch."

"Being in control is rather empowering." Dainty hands settled on his hips before venturing to the waistband of his breeches.

"What now, Lilly?"

"I have no idea."

Fabian smiled. "While I'm keen to see where your fingers might wander next, I'm afraid I must remove my boots."

She glanced at his feet, her gaze lingering on the obvious

evidence of his arousal. It seemed to give her confidence in her ability, as she said, "Then hurry."

Why was it that a desperate man's fingers failed to work? After three attempts, he yanked one boot free and then another. Fabian had never been shy of nakedness. That's what came from living amongst fifty sailors for months on end. He unbuttoned his breeches but left them hanging on his hips. The last thing he wanted was to frighten his wife away.

Sensing her increasing nerves, he closed the gap between them. "May I have an opportunity to explore, too?"

With some hesitation, Lillian nodded.

Keeping his eyes locked on hers, Fabian bent his knees, found the hem of her chemise and ran his hands underneath. Lillian inhaled deeply as he skimmed her soft thighs.

"You can kiss me if the urge takes you," he whispered as he cupped her buttocks.

Lillian's breath came quickly as he caressed the flare of her hips and palmed her full breasts. He rejoiced in the glazed look of desire swimming in her eyes, in the little pants she couldn't contain. While he lived and breathed, he'd make sure she had no reason to cry again.

Good God. Lust clawed away like a beast inside. His cock bulged against his breeches, and all he could think of was pushing into her sweet body.

How he had the strength to rein in his desire, he'd never know. But Lillian needed to surrender to him, to embrace her passionate nature, to learn how to feel something other than guilt and shame.

He pushed his breeches to the floor and stepped out of them. Giving her no time to think, he gathered her to his chest and plundered her mouth. One stroke of his tongue across the seam of her lips and she granted him entrance. Things progressed quickly.

She clutched his arms, scratching his skin in her need to deepen the kiss.

Fabian continued to devour her mouth while his fingers moved to the hem of her chemise and edged it up to her waist.

"Raise your arms." He did not give her an opportunity to protest but lifted the garment over her head and threw it onto the bed.

"Fabian—"

He covered her mouth again, thrust inside with his tongue while pressing his erection against her abdomen. Oh, he would love nothing more than to stand and admire her body, admire God's perfection. But he needed to feel her come apart in his hands, to shudder and cry out his name.

With nimble fingers, he traced a path down to the intimate place between her thighs and stroked gently back and forth. He swallowed down her tiny gasps, sounds that quickly turned into sweet moans.

Lillian clutched his waist, pulling him, urging him to give her something more.

Fabian backed her towards the bed. All the while her frantic hands caressed his bare skin. Without warning, he scooped her up into his arms and placed her down on top of the coverlet. Lord, his wife was lush and ripe for the taking.

"You're sure you want to do this?" He'd ripped her away from her home, persuaded her to marry him. Was it too late to act the gentleman now?

Lillian nodded and blinked rapidly. For a second, her glazed eyes held a hint of fear. "Kiss me, Fabian, before I start to remember all the reasons why I should be frightened."

Needing no further inducement, Fabian climbed onto the bed and rose above her. "Oh, I intend to kiss you, just not in the places you expect."

The glorious rise and fall of her breasts drew his attention. He could have gazed upon them all night, but the urge to take her nipple in his mouth forced him to bend his head. He flicked his tongue across the tip, traced circles, sucked and nipped until Lillian's embarrassment evaporated and she arched her back, pushing her breast against his mouth.

Eager to rouse a cry of ecstasy from her lips, Fabian moved lower. He rained kisses all the way down to her navel. While Lillian hummed with pleasure, he gripped her knees and bent her legs, then delved lower to press his lips to her most intimate place.

"Fabian." His name came on a gasp. "Wait."

But he didn't wait; he'd waited too long for this woman. For years, he'd imagined this moment, and he had every intention of bringing it to its rightful conclusion.

"Hush, love. Trust me. You must learn to let go." He lavished her swollen sex with attention.

With the swirl of his tongue, her breath came in short, fast pants. "Fabian." She thrust her hands into his hair, holding him in position.

The sweet scent of her arousal sent his own desire spiralling. And then the dam burst. The tremors of her climax shook her body. She gasped and cried out as her legs shuddered with pleasure. With a firm hold of his hair, she urged him to rise above her.

One glance at his solid cock and she swallowed deeply. "Now, Fabian. Do it now. Don't wait."

Her words were music to his ears. A delicious fever consumed him mind and body as he took himself in hand and nudged at her entrance.

This was it—time to claim the only woman he'd ever wanted. He pushed inside her. The muscles in her core welcomed him, hugged his cock so tightly he could feel the power of the intimate embrace deep in his chest.

He stilled, relishing the feel of her muscles clamped around him. Ever so slowly he withdrew, rolled his hips and thrust inside her again. Lillian's mouth opened on a moan. Each drive home flamed the fire burning in his veins.

"God, you're perfect," he panted. Joining with her was everything he thought it would be, and more. "I promise your life will be filled with pleasure from now on."

She gripped his buttocks in response, dug her fingers into his flesh and urged him to quicken the pace. He obliged, entering her over and over, so hard, so deep. Damn, he'd struggle to last more than a minute. Possessed by a craving he couldn't quite comprehend, he sheathed himself in her warmth, her wetness, encouraged her to buck her hips and writhe to draw his climax from him.

His body shook and pulsed with the power of it.

For the first time in his life, he did not withdraw but gave his wife everything of himself. Perhaps a child. Perhaps hope for the future.

CHAPTER ELEVEN

The sound of their ragged breathing filled the room. Lillian lay naked, delicious tingles still coursing through her body. Fabian lay beside her, one leg draped over her thigh, one arm resting heavily across her stomach. An inner calm filled her chest. One that spoke of more than physical satisfaction. Fabian had kept his promise. In that one blissful moment, she had indeed felt free.

"The next time we explore the realms of intimate relations, I hope to dedicate more time to enhancing your pleasure." Fabian's husky voice caressed her senses. He came up on his elbow, a satisfied smile playing at the corners of his mouth. "What do you say? Would you care to put my skill to the test?"

"What, now?" Although a warm shiver raced down her spine at the prospect, she had promised to tell him the truth about Lord Martin. The longer she delayed, the more daunting the task.

"Not right now." He placed the tip of his finger on her chin and traced a slow, sensual line all the way down to her navel. The mischievous glint in his eyes simmered to a heated smoulder. "We have time for a drink, and I need to stoke the fire."

Part of her wanted to indulge him. When they were alone, when he kissed her, she forgot anyone or anything else existed.

"And I do need to thank you for saving my life," he added. "I trust you meant to blow the blade out of Aubrey's hand."

"Aubrey? Is that his name?"

"Apparently so."

"Somehow, he doesn't seem so terrifying now."

"You appeared quite calm when you pulled the trigger. Where did you learn to shoot like that?"

"Vane insisted I take lessons." Oh, how she wished she'd had the skill to fight a duel with Lord Martin. She would have hit him between the legs to prevent him from taking another woman for a fool.

"Then for once, I owe your brother my gratitude."

"What did you do with him?"

Fabian frowned. "With whom? Vane?"

"No, the man with the pockmarked face." He didn't deserve to be called by his name.

"He's in the dungeon for the time being. Mackenzie is looking after him." Fabian fell silent, though she could feel his gaze drifting over her breasts before lingering on her locket. "Must you wear the necklace to bed?"

The question shocked her. It would be easy to lie. But she'd reached the point in her life where nothing but the truth would do. "As long as I live, I shall never take it off."

"I see." Suspicion lingered within those two simple words. "I suppose it is too much to hope that you carry your mother's portrait."

"While I loved my mother, it is not her likeness I hold dear."

A sigh left his lips. "While it pains me to ask, did you develop an attachment to Lord Martin?"

One did not need the wisdom of Socrates to know what he

was really asking. Had she married *him* despite loving someone else? "No. While I carried a mild affection for him, one I believed might blossom into something more, I did not love him."

"But you do love the person whose likeness you keep close to your heart?"

"I do." A surge of raw emotion filled her chest. Tears stung her eyes and threatened to fall. "I have never known a love like it."

Fabian sat up and thrust his hand through his hair. "If you love another, then why marry me? Is it not better to be a spinster, to stay true to oneself rather than live a lie?"

"I think you're suffering from a terrible misconception." The lump in her throat grew so large she struggled to swallow. She pinched the end of her nose to stem the flood waters. "It—it is not a gentleman's portrait I carry."

Fabian turned to face her, confusion marring his brow. "Please tell me it's not a picture of your brother."

The comment pricked her ire. "Don't be ridiculous. You're not listening to what I'm saying."

"Is it ridiculous? Vane is practically your shadow."

Anger and a gut-wrenching pain consumed her. She jumped out of bed, found her chemise, thrust it over her head and tugged the material to her knees.

"It's on the wrong way round."

Lillian glanced down but was past the point of caring. Feeling somewhat less vulnerable now the garment covered her modesty, she placed her hands on her hips. "Let me make one thing clear. Vane is a kind, loving brother who will do anything to secure my happiness. But it is not his memory I cling to."

"Then whose is it?" His tone conveyed more than a hint of jealousy. Had the lord of the seas developed a sense of inferiority? "What hope do we have of moving beyond the past if you cannot be honest with me? We have all lived with loss."

"To lose a loved one is distressing." It felt like having her heart ripped from her chest while it was still beating. "But to lose a child ... there is no greater pain."

The dam holding her emotions at bay burst. Tears cascaded down her face and dripped from her chin.

Fabian stared at her, his eyes wide with shock. "You ... you lost a child?" He covered his mouth with his hand.

She tried to speak, but a whimper escaped. The whimper became a sob. "I lost a daughter, Fabian. I lost the most beautiful —" Her knees buckled, and she fell to the floor.

Fabian was at her side in seconds. Strong arms enveloped her. He pulled her into his lap and cradled her as the wail of a soul-deep loss echoed through the chamber.

She could not express her grief in front of Vane. Seeing pain and guilt flare in her brother's eyes only made matters worse.

"Hush, love." Fabian stroked her hair, kissed her forehead and rocked her gently back and forth. "Forgive me for pressing you on the subject, but know you do not have to suffer in silence."

Lillian wrapped her arms around him so tightly she feared she might squeeze all the air from his lungs. Touching him should have felt awkward and new, yet it felt so comforting, so familiar. She buried her face in his neck. Just like everything else about him, the scent of his skin helped to ease her torment.

"You can tell me about Lord Martin when you're ready," he whispered. "It doesn't have to be now."

Whenever she thought about the scoundrel, about all that happened in Italy, inside she became a shivering wreck. Fabian now knew her darkest secret, and it had not altered his opinion of her. A part of her loved him for that. It was time to trust him, time to tell him everything.

Lillian sucked in a breath and looked up at her husband. "Let us sit by the fire and drink brandy." That would banish the chill from her bones. "I shall tell you about Lord Martin, and of my daughter, Charlotte."

Saying her name aloud validated her daughter's existence. It confirmed she was real, the only good thing to come from a horrid nightmare.

Fabian kissed her forehead. "Only if you want to. Only if you feel able."

"I do."

Fabian helped her to her feet and guided her over to the chair. She sat and watched him dress quickly, stoke the fire and pour the drinks. Two glasses in hand, he returned to sit opposite.

"To friendship." He offered her a glass and raised his in salute. "Life has not been kind but know you can trust me, Lilly."

"To friendship." Liquid fire trickled down her throat as she took the first few sips. "Know that despite my reservations, I do not regret marrying you."

He put his hand over his heart. "After the way I behaved, that is a compliment indeed."

A nervous silence ensued.

He cradled his glass and stared at the dancing flames in the hearth.

"I won't bore you with the minor details," she finally found the courage to say. "Perhaps it will be easier just to relay the facts."

He nodded but said nothing.

"Lord Martin paid me court for a month before he offered marriage. During that time, he convinced me of his affection, and I believed him to be a kind and generous gentleman."

"And your brother approved of the match?"

She snorted. In Vane's eyes, no one was good enough. "Not at first. He insisted upon checking Martin's background. Other than a penchant for gambling, people held him in high regard."

"Gambling? Surely that was enough to convince Vane the

man lacked merit. It takes a weak man to squander three generations of hard-earned funds."

"The debts were small, infrequent, paid on time." A blush rose to her cheeks. Fabian was right. It was a warning sign they'd failed to take seriously. Yet another reason why Vane blamed himself. "As the wedding drew closer, he began acting strangely, demanding to know if I loved him."

"But you didn't."

"No. And I couldn't lie." She'd been tactful, told him love blossomed over time. "I told him I cared for him and knew it would develop into something more."

"I have never met Lord Martin, but he sounds like an insecure fop."

"Oh, he was so kind to me, Fabian. We talked for hours about music and poetry. There are not many men who value a lady's opinion."

He sipped his brandy, all the while watching her over the rim of his glass.

"Obviously, he stole a kiss whenever the opportunity arose. But one night, he asked me to meet him in the summerhouse at the bottom of the garden. He said he needed a commitment from me, a token gesture to cement our alliance."

Fabian gritted his teeth. "What you speak of is a common ploy of a seducer."

"Indeed." Oh, what a naive fool she'd been. It pained her to think of it now.

"I trust Vane knew nothing of the lord's plans."

"No, not at the time." She sighed. "And I'm sure I don't need to explain what happened." She'd been out of her depth, floundering in uncharted waters. When one swam with sharks, one rarely surfaced unscathed. "The next day Lord Martin broke our engagement and boarded the first ship to France."

Fabian's countenance darkened. "And so Vane chased him all

the way to Italy and put a ball in his chest. One can hardly blame him."

"No. Well … yes. We followed him. Oh, Vane wanted to string him up from the nearest bough, wanted to put a ball between his brows. But I begged him to show clemency. They fought a duel. Lord Martin fired and missed and so Vane shot him in the leg."

Fabian straightened. "One rarely dies from a leg wound."

"Lord Martin died from a fever, as a result of the wound."

"Vane was too accommodating."

She'd wanted to see Lord Martin suffer, too. Nonetheless, she could not let Vane kill a man for her mistake.

"We stayed in Italy for obvious reasons." This was the part she needed to say quickly. "Vane rented a house overlooking the bay in Naples. A pretty place with an abundance of lemon trees. Charlotte was born. She was two months old when she passed peacefully in her sleep. We stayed for some time afterwards, but Vane wanted to come home."

In truth, she had found it hard to leave. She bent her head and kissed the locket. It was a silly gesture that eased her pain.

Fabian sat motionless in the chair. His intense, unblinking stare unnerved her. "If Lord Martin were alive, I would gut him like a pig and trail his innards around Berkeley Square."

"Then I'm thankful he is not. The stench from the river is bad enough."

A heavy silence hung in the air.

"I need another drink." Fabian stood, refilled his glass and returned to his seat. "The question is what does Lord Cornell have to do with it all?"

This was where she really had been a blind fool.

"Someone bribed Lord Martin to ruin me," she said coldly. "Apparently, someone tricked him into gambling away his home and fortune. In return for blackening my name, all vowels were destroyed."

"But why would someone do that?"

"To hurt my brother. I'm afraid Vane's love for me is his only weakness." She gestured to the room. "A fact you have also used to your advantage."

He flopped back in the chair, almost spilling his brandy. A haunted look marred his handsome countenance. "Do not compare me to those men."

She hadn't meant to, but when one behaved selfishly, one had to be held to account. "I am merely demonstrating that I am Vane's Achilles heel. In that respect, he will always be vulnerable."

The glow of the fire's flames went some way to banishing the sudden chill in the air. Fabian stared at the amber liquid in the glass, swirled it around and watched it settle. Eventually, he looked at her.

"There is one vast difference." The words were slow and measured. "Lord Martin cared nothing for you, that much is clear."

"And you do?" She could not keep the cynical edge from her tone.

Fabian drained the glass and stood. He offered her his hand. "Come, the hour is late, and you've had a tiring day. You need sleep. We will discuss Lord Cornell's involvement once we have more facts."

Lillian gripped his fingers and came to her feet. "I cannot drink this." She offered him the glass. He took it and finished what remained before placing the empty vessels on the side table.

"Sleep in here tonight." Fabian moved to the bed and drew back the coverlet. "It's warm and more comfortable."

A vision of their passionate lovemaking flashed into her mind, and the need to feel close to him came upon her again. Feeling his large, warm body next to hers would bring comfort during the long night ahead. Sleep always eluded her when her mind was full of memories of the past.

"I suppose I should straighten my chemise." Dismissing her embarrassment, she eased her arms out of the garment, turned it the right way and thrust her arms back into the sleeves. "Does it matter which side I sleep on?"

A weak smile touched his lips. "No, not tonight."

"Good, then I shall take the right-hand side."

He watched her climb into bed, came to stand beside her and pulled the sheets up around her shoulders. With a sigh, he stroked a lock of hair from her cheek. "Sleep well."

His awkward stance unnerved her. "Are you not joining me?"

He bent down and kissed her on the lips, a tender and gentle display of affection that sang to her soul. "Rest assured, when I return I shall lavish you with the attention you deserve."

The muscles in her core pulsed at the prospect. "Return? Have the night's activities left you famished?" Hours had passed since he'd eaten at the banquet. "Call for a cold platter. I'm sure there was food left from the feast."

"While I have a huge appetite, that is not the reason I must leave."

Leave? The word carried an air of finality, suggested a lengthy separation. It was as though someone had punched a hole in her stomach and wrung the muscles tight. "Am I allowed to ask where you're going?"

"There is an urgent matter that requires my attention."

"And you did not think to mention it before?" Despite his affectionate manner, his eyes were a hard, obsidian black. Since telling her story, she'd sensed a suppressed tension that was in no way aimed at her. "Are you leaving the island?"

He inclined his head. "I shall be back in a few days. In my

absence, everyone will look to you for guidance. Mackenzie will assist you."

"You're going to London." It was a statement, not a question.

"I have business there. We will discuss the matter upon my return." He did not give her an opportunity to object, but removed a few items of clothing from the armoire, bowed respectfully and marched out of the room.

CHAPTER TWELVE

"Forgive me, my lady. It's not my place to question your instructions, but his lordship will have my hide if he knows I left you alone with the prisoner." With a grimace, Mackenzie's gaze shifted between Lillian and her new maid, Mary.

"I am not asking for your permission, Mackenzie." Fear forced Lillian to speak in the stern voice of a matron. She had to know if the rogue had an accomplice. "We have no notion when his lordship will return, but I demand access to the dungeon so I may question this Aubrey fellow."

The hollow ache in her stomach returned. Four days had passed since she'd told Fabian her story. Every day, she climbed to the roof of the keep and stared out to sea. Watching. Waiting. Praying he was not lying in a watery grave. Every night, she slept in Fabian's bed, inhaling the scent of the man who commanded her every waking thought, visited her in her dreams, too.

"The dungeons are no place for a lady." Mackenzie squirmed on the spot.

"Then bring the prisoner to the great hall, and I shall question him there." For the last two nights, she'd watched the strange goings-on from the bedchamber window, seen the light swaying to and fro in the distance.

"Please, my lady, listen to reason." Mackenzie made an odd puffing sound. "His lordship will flay me alive if anything happens to you. Is there no compromise? Will you not allow me to accompany you?"

There were other questions she wanted to ask, and she would rather have no witnesses. Lord Cornell's desire for vengeance was great indeed else he would have been content with her ruination. She had to know why Cornell wanted to hurt Vane.

"Aubrey can do me no harm. Words do not hurt." The lack of conviction in Lillian's tone was evident. One man's comments could not penetrate her steely reserve, and yet a barrage of snide whispers proved as painful as being pelted with pebbles. "But you may accompany me as far as the steps."

"Will you not allow *me* to question the prisoner?"

Mary sighed. "Mackenzie, have you not heard what your mistress said?"

The Scot's eyes softened whenever he gazed upon the fiery-haired woman at Lillian's side. Since hearing about the men's distrust of Doyle's wife, Lillian had welcomed Mary to the castle. From the woman's caring and friendly manner, one would suspect she had a heart as large as Mackenzie's.

"Can I help it if I want to protect the lass?" Mackenzie implored.

Mary stepped forward and placed a hand on his arm. "We will wait at the bottom of the steps, and keep Lady Ravenscroft in our sights at all times." Mary cast a sidelong glance, looking for Lillian's approval.

"What I have to say to Aubrey is a private matter." She would ask about Vane. Had Aubrey seen him during those chaotic hours at Vauxhall? A vision of her brother's frightened face entered her mind. He must be beside himself with worry. "But you can wait with Mary."

Mackenzie nodded, and his gaze flicked to the dainty hand still resting on his sleeve. "I have the key in my pocket." He tapped his chest. "Shall we head there now and get this matter over with?"

Mary's hand slipped from Mackenzie's sleeve. "You'll need a cloak, my lady. Shall I fetch the one Ursula found for you?"

Having arrived at the island with nothing but the clothes on her back, Nancy and Ursula had begged and borrowed the necessary items to last until alternative arrangements were made.

"Thank you, Mary. We will wait for you here."

They watched Mary hurry away.

"Mary has been your shadow for the last few days," Mackenzie said. "Offering her work at the castle shows the men they've nothing to fear. For that, I'm eternally grateful to you, lass."

"Her husband has abandoned her, and I've never been one to condemn a person for someone else's mistake."

Mackenzie inclined his head respectfully. "Happen that's why his lordship is besotted with you."

A weak chuckle escaped. "His lordship married me out of necessity. Surely you know that."

"I'm not so sure. From the tales he's told, I'd say he's admired you since you were a girl. He said that you once told him that it's not the stars that hold one's destiny but ourselves."

Lillian's heart skipped a beat. "I did say that, although I cannot claim the credit for Shakespeare's wise words."

"Either way, his lordship holds your opinion in high regard."

"We were friends once." During which time she hoped for more. She'd thought of him many times over the years. Would things have been different were it not for his father's poor investment? "And perhaps we've found a way to become friends again."

"Friends?" Mackenzie raised a brow. "After the way his lordship kissed you, I'd say there's more to it than that."

A blush warmed her cold cheeks. They *were* more than friends. She'd felt an intense burst of affection for him the moment he entered her body. "Oh, Mackenzie, do you think he's all right?" The panic she'd kept at bay for days erupted. "What if he's had an accident? What if he's hurt?"

Mackenzie pursed his lips and patted her arm. "There now, lass. His lordship has sailed the worst storms I've ever had the misfortune to witness and lived to tell the tale. And he's got Freddie Fortune with him. The man's a walking monument to luck." Mackenzie gave a sly wink. "Although I imagine his lordship took Freddie along to make use of his light fingers if you take my meaning."

Was this what it felt like to be a sailor's wife? Four days felt like a lifetime. The agonising wait proved all-consuming. How had she gone from wanting to punch Fabian for dragging her to the desolate island to wanting to feel cocooned in his warm embrace?

"I need a distraction, Mackenzie." Errant thoughts filled her head. Would Fabian be different when he returned? After listening to her story, did he think less of her than before? Good Lord. These strange emotions had turned her into a wreck. "I need something to occupy my mind while he's gone."

"Leave it to me. If it's a distraction you seek, I know just the thing. These men are adept at keeping themselves entertained during long voyages."

Mary returned to the bailey, clutching a dark blue cloak. "Here, my lady, this should keep the chill at bay." Mary was as attentive as Mackenzie. She draped the garment around Lillian's shoulders and fastened the ties at the collar as if Lillian were incapable of performing the task herself.

With a look of wonder, Mackenzie studied Mary's red hair but then caught himself and mumbled incoherently. "We'd better see what that dirty beggar has to say for himself."

"Then lead the way."

A narrow flight of steps gave access to the dungeon. Mackenzie insisted on descending first. Perhaps he thought to scare away the rats, or to seek confirmation that the prisoner hadn't escaped during the night.

The temperature plummeted. The putrid stench in the air, a disgusting concoction of faeces, sweat and stagnant water, assaulted her nostrils. The urge to retch proved great.

"I trust you've given the man a chamber pot." Lillian put her hand to her mouth as it brought much-needed relief. "This is not medieval England after all."

"Aye, we've afforded him every luxury." Mackenzie coughed to hide a chuckle.

Lillian stared down the dim corridor. A torch flickered in the sconce, casting eerie shadows over the damp walls.

"Are you sure you don't want me to accompany you, lass?"

Mary tutted. She'd chastised Mackenzie numerous times for his familiarity. "Yes, *my lady*, I can walk by your side if it pleases you."

A low moan drifted through the darkness, followed by the loud clank of metal hitting metal. It echoed through the cramped chamber like a death knell.

"You Scottish bastard, let me out of this damn cage." The gruff voice came from a chamber further along the corridor. "Show yourself." The clanging continued.

"I swear I shall whip that man's bahooky with a birch if he doesn't keep his filthy mouth shut," Mackenzie muttered through gritted teeth. He turned to Lillian. "Don't go down there, my lady."

Lillian squared her shoulders. "I shall be fine. The man is behind bars. It was never his intention to do me harm, only to spy."

"Och, I doubt the Devil himself could deter you from your course when you've got your mind set."

"Did Lord Ravenscroft not tell you? The Sandfords are known for their stubbornness and impatience." Gathering her courage, Lillian began her slow march towards the cell. She ignored the squeaking and scuttling to her left. If she screamed, Mackenzie would come running.

"Do you hear me?" Aubrey shouted.

Lillian drew closer. The orange glow from the torch cast a dim light over the figure standing at the cell door. The iron poles were the only thing preventing the rogue escaping.

Gnarled hands gripped the bars and tried to shake them loose. "Highlander? Come show me your pretty skirt."

"It's not Mackenzie." Lillian came to a halt outside the prison but remained more than an arm's length away. "It is Lady Ravenscroft."

Aubrey pressed his scarred face to the bars. Purple bruises lined his eyes and his nose looked crooked. The ugly snarl vanished. "Please, my lady, tell them to release me. There are rats and insects aplenty down here, and a man can't sleep on a damp floor."

The man should have thought about that before he came trespassing. "I'm afraid you must wait until my husband returns. He alone has the power to release you."

Aubrey's nostrils flared, and he shook the bars so violently one could imagine him wringing a person's neck with ease.

"But if you answer my questions," Lillian continued, "I shall do what I can to persuade Lord Ravenscroft to set you free."

"What good is that? I could be locked in here for months."

"He's expected back in the next day or so." The lie helped to allay her fears. "My brother is also due to arrive soon, and let me tell you, he is not as forgiving as the Raven."

"Trevane?" Aubrey's eyes widened. "Trevane is coming here?"

"Indeed. I don't imagine he will look favourably upon your actions." She didn't care how Vane dealt with Aubrey, but her brother was liable to fly into an uncontrollable rage when he discovered the extent of her duplicity.

"And if I answer your questions will you tell Trevane I helped you?"

"Yes."

"What do you want to know?"

"Did you come here with an accomplice?" She couldn't shake the feeling that someone lurked out on the heathland. Perhaps it was nothing, just one of Fabian's men walking with a lamp. Still, she should mention it to Mackenzie. "I doubt you rowed all the way from the mainland single-handedly."

"I could row to France and it would be no hardship," Aubrey grunted. "And I ain't got no accomplice. I work alone."

"If you're lying, I cannot plead for your release."

"I ain't no rich man. Only a fool shares his bounty, and his lordship don't want the whole world knowing his business."

Probably because Lord Cornell didn't want anyone to know he was a heartless coward. "Why does Lord Cornell want to hurt my brother?"

Aubrey shrugged. "It has something to do with his wife, but that's all I know."

Vane was a man with a voracious appetite for carnal pleasures. It was his way of erasing the pain caused by Estelle's death, Lillian knew that. But since Lord Martin's deception, her brother had shied away from all illicit liaisons.

"And how long has Cornell held this grudge?"

"A few years, I don't doubt, though he only hired me when you came back to London."

"Has he hired anyone else to snoop into our affairs?"

"How should I know?"

"Did Cornell mention how he plans to hurt my brother?" Like all weak men, it would not be a direct attack.

"I'm just paid to tell him of your whereabouts, to follow you wherever you go. Lucky I made it as far as Branscombe. The fishermen thought I was one of the Raven's men and pointed me in the right direction."

Well, she'd learnt nothing new about Lord Cornell. Still, it had passed the time while she waited for Fabian to return.

Lillian cleared her throat. "I have just one more question."

"Then let's hear it."

Pressing her lips firmly together, she hesitated. Did she really need to know the answer to the question that had plagued her for days? "You said you saw my brother at Vauxhall. How did he seem?" It was a ridiculous question, but she had no one else to ask.

"Seem?" Aubrey frowned.

"Did he look distraught?"

"Haunted more like. He looked like a man who'd lost everything on the turn of the dice."

Her stomach flipped as another bout of nausea took hold. "What was he doing?"

"Ain't that enough questions for one day?"

"Please." She stepped forward. "Just tell me what you saw."

"He was the last to leave Vauxhall, hung around the gate for twenty minutes, marching back and forth like a man fit for Bedlam. He dragged every passer-by aside, waving his arms and pointing to the Pleasure Gardens. Almost throttled one man he did."

Oh, Vane.

The solid lump in her throat made it hard to breathe.

In a sudden move, Aubrey stretched his hand through the bars and tugged on her cloak. "Now get me out of this blasted hole."

Lillian stumbled back and wrenched the material from his grasp. "As I said, I shall speak to my husband upon his return." Despite Aubrey's shouts and jeers to open the cell door, she turned away and hurried back to Mackenzie.

"Pay him no mind, my lady." Mackenzie stepped forward, took her arm and led her to the steps. "Did you get the information you needed?"

"Aubrey answered my questions." She wiped a tear from her eye. "Though I'm certain it was not at all what I needed."

"If that rogue has said anything to upset you I'll—"

"No, Mackenzie." Lillian raised her hand. "He told me only what I suspected." She needed to clear her mind, to breathe clean air, and so hurried up the steps and burst through the open door leading to the bailey.

Guilt wrapped around her heart like a vine. It was only right she put Vane out of his misery, only right that she offer an explanation. She would wait one more day for Fabian before heading back to London.

Sensing Mackenzie's presence behind her, she swung around. "Did Lord Ravenscroft not give you any indication when he would return?"

"No, my lady, though I'm sure it's not his intention to stay away any longer than necessary."

"Then if he does not return tomorrow, I must insist a few men escort me to London."

"London?" Mackenzie cried. Two men filling buckets from the well stopped and stared. "His lordship gave me the job of keeping you safe, and I cannot do that if you're away from here."

"I know you take your obligation seriously. Indeed, is that

why you have men roaming the heathland at night with their lanterns?" She paused upon noting his confused expression.

Mackenzie straightened to his full height. "What makes you say that?"

"Have you not sent a man out these last two nights to patrol the area? I have seen him pacing outside the wall holding his lantern aloft."

A tense silence ensued.

"I've given no such orders." Mackenzie rubbed his forehead. "Are you sure you're not mistaken?"

"I know what I saw." Doubt surfaced. She had stood at the window and stared into the night for far too long. It was true. She imagined seeing Vane striding towards the castle, had played the scene over in her mind. What would she say to him? How would he react?

"Perhaps you saw one of the men returning to the dock," Mary suggested.

Mackenzie frowned. "No one was to leave or enter the grounds without my knowledge. Unless——" He swung around and glared at the men carrying buckets of water, and at those brushing down the horses. "If one of those blighters has been out digging for treasure, I shall——"

"Treasure?" Lillian thought she'd misheard.

"Can you take me to where you saw them?"

"Certainly." Curiosity outweighed any anxious feelings she might have had.

"Shall I wait here, Mackenzie?" Mary asked.

"You'd better come, too." Mackenzie gestured to the gates leading from the bailey.

Lillian led the way out of the gatehouse and towards the vast expanse of heathland. Purple sprigs of heather, bright yellow flowers and tufts of green made for a vibrant carpet in the daytime. Raising the hem of her dress, she navigated the terrain, stopping only when they reached the area with a clear view of her bedchamber window.

"The light hovered around here before moving left and then ahead again." Glancing back and forth between the window and the heath, she pointed to a spot in the distance. "It lingered over there for a time."

Mackenzie trudged past her, scouring the ground, kicking at plants with the toe of his boot.

"The folks in Branscombe say there's treasure hidden somewhere on this island," Mary said as they watched Mackenzie pace back and forth like a bloodhound searching for a scent. "Brought ashore during the Armada. Lord Ravenscroft told the men it's just a tale, said he'd banish anyone caught digging. In all the time I've lived here, I've never known a man disobey the master's orders."

Lillian considered what Fabian had told her about Doyle. Mary had made no mention of her husband during the few days she'd been working at the castle. "And yet your husband did."

Mary shuffled nervously. She drew her cloak across her chest and gripped the edges. "When a man is too stupid to count his blessings then there's no hope for him."

"Have you heard from your husband since Lord Ravenscroft banished him?"

Mary blinked rapidly and shook her head. "No, my lady, the man never considered me a priority. But I thank the Lord we've no children. Else it would have given him a reason to return."

Lillian understood the woman's logic more than most. Still, trust was not something she gave freely—not anymore. And while she wanted to believe Mary spoke the truth, she struggled to accept her word.

"Should you see your husband you must inform Lord Ravenscroft at once."

Mary nodded. "And thank you, my lady, for giving me a

position in your household. Things have been hard these last few months, and I welcome your assistance."

"It is Mackenzie you must thank. The man sings your praises and was keen to help now you're on your own."

"I knew it!" Mackenzie shouted. "Unless the rabbits have learnt to use a shovel, someone has been digging."

Mary's eyes lit up when she gazed at the figure on his knees examining the plants. "There's no man in the world as kind as Mackenzie."

Lillian's thoughts turned to Fabian. Despite bringing her to the island against her will, every deed and gesture spoke of a kind heart, too. But what husband left his wife on their wedding night? What could be so important to keep him away from home for days?

CHAPTER THIRTEEN

Woken by a noise in her chamber, Lillian opened her eyes and stared out into the darkness. She was too afraid to move, too afraid to give the figure creeping past her line of vision any indication she was awake. Her first instinct had been to jump out of bed and call Fabian's name. But the initial flurry of excitement vanished when she realised the person was too short to be her husband, too slight of frame to be the prisoner, Aubrey.

Lillian cursed silently. Why in heaven's name had she not slept with her pistol? The cock of the hammer would be enough to frighten the intruder away.

She watched the figure take a book off the side table, grab the spine and shake it before picking another one and doing the same. Book in hand, the figure froze and focused his attention on the bed. How she kept her breathing calm she would never know.

Believing Lillian still slept, he moved to the armoire. The loud creak of the door forced him to abandon his search there. What was he looking for? What was he hoping to find?

Only when he moved past the window did Lillian suspect the intruder was a woman. Her gait lacked strength and confidence. Shrouded in a black cloak with the hood raised, the trespasser crept about the room, clearly looking for something specific. The wooden chest captured her attention. She opened the box carefully, her fingers gliding over whatever was inside.

The urge to discover the woman's identity burned in Lillian's chest, and so she chose that moment to strike.

Leaping out of bed as though the coverlet had caught fire, she charged forward and grabbed the woman around the waist. "What in God's name are you doing in here?" Lillian held on as the woman tried to wriggle free of her grasp. "Show yourself."

The intruder groaned as she struggled but did not utter a word.

Lillian tried to pull the hood down, to reveal some identifying feature, but the woman fought like a wildcat against Lillian's grasp. They both battled for control, but then the woman grabbed something from the chest and swung it back over her shoulder.

"Ouch!" The metal object caught Lillian on the upper arm, again just above her brow. The impact took her legs from beneath her, and she crumpled into a heap on the floor.

The woman made a hasty retreat. She was out of the door and running along the corridor before Lillian caught her breath. Scrambling to her feet, Lillian hurried to the open door and peered into the darkness. Despite the pain above her left eye she had every intention of following in pursuit, but a drop of blood landed on her white chemise, then another, and another.

A muttered curse fell from her lips.

Blood stained her fingers when she dabbed the skin above her brow. The pain made her wince. With nothing to stem the bleeding, she gathered up the hem of her chemise and pressed the material to the cut.

From the window, she watched the intruder sneak out through the bailey. The figure moved across the heathland towards the faint flicker of light in the distance. It was too late to charge out into the night. Still, she should alert Mackenzie.

To get to the Scot's quarters, she had to go through the tower door and along another corridor. As she had no notion which room was his, all she could do was call out his name.

"Mackenzie?" Lillian came to the first door and knocked. "Mackenzie, can you hear me?" She hammered the door with her fist when no one answered.

A bang and clatter echoed from a room at the far end of the corridor. A deep groan accompanied a mumbled curse. The door flew open, and Mackenzie darted out into the hall wearing a shirt and breeches.

"Is that you, my lady?" He brushed his hand over his unkempt hair as he peered at her through the gloom.

"Mackenzie." His name escaped in a breathless pant.

The Scot came to stand before her, a look of horror marring his features. "For all the saints! What happened to your eye?" His frantic gaze swept over the cloak she'd thrown around her shoulders to protect her modesty, then fell to the blood stains on her chemise.

Lillian drew the cloak across her body. "Someone came into my room. She searched the books and rummaged through the chest, though I have no notion what she was looking for."

"She? A woman did this to you?" He narrowed his gaze, examining the cut above her brow. "May I take a closer look?"

Lillian nodded. "I waited until she turned her back and then I grabbed her from behind. She swung around and hit me with a metal object, a candlestick I think, but she took it with her when she ran."

"Och, you may need a stitch or two. And it looks like you might have a scar."

Mackenzie was more concerned with her injury than the fact someone had assaulted her. "Did you hear me, Mackenzie? Someone stole into my room with less than honourable intentions."

"Aye, lass, I heard you." Mackenzie sighed. "And we'll get to that in a minute, but first we must decide what to do about this."

"Are you not the least bit curious who it might be?"

"Forgive me, lass, but I'm having a mighty old time controlling my temper. Give me a minute else I'm liable to tear the place apart and throttle every person fool enough to step in my way. And I don't want to think about what his lordship will do when he sees —" Mackenzie stopped abruptly, closed his eyes and exhaled.

"There's little point concerning yourself with that now," she said to calm the man. "And is it not better to wait a while before making a decision about stitching the wound?"

Mackenzie opened his eyes and glanced at the cut. "We will see what Mrs Hill says when she looks at it. Now, you're certain the rogue was a woman?"

"Yes, though it was dark and she'd raised the hood on her cloak to hide her identity."

"What about her voice?"

"Other than a few grunts and groans, she never spoke."

"And you have no idea what she wanted?"

"No." The image of the woman shaking the books entered her mind. "Although I suspect it's something small, a letter or some other document."

"With your permission, my lady, I would like to escort you back to your room. I shall send Mrs Hill to examine your injury while I make a thorough search of the castle."

"Very well, but it will be a wasted effort. I watched the woman leave through the bailey. She met someone out on the heath."

Mackenzie gritted his teeth. "I'd hate to be the traitor who has to stand before the Raven and answer for his crimes."

Lillian's heart lurched whenever anyone mentioned Fabian. The longer he stayed away, the more she craved his company.

"One thing is certain. From her shapely curves, the woman was most definitely not Mrs Bell, Nancy Hill or Penny." As the words left her lips, she knew her attacker could only be one of three people: Heather, Ursula or Mary. They were all of a similar height and build, although Lillian had given Mary permission to return to her cottage for the night.

"That leaves but a few possible suspects. Whoever it is had better be running for the hills."

After putting on his boots, Mackenzie walked Lillian to her chamber and went to find Mrs Hill. The woman came with a pot that smelt of honey and smeared the contents over the wound.

"I doubt you'll need it stitched, and with this here ointment there's little chance of it leaving a scar."

A knock at the door brought Mackenzie. "Well, do I need to get my needle and thread?"

"Why don't we wait and see how it is in the morning?" Nancy said. "No point causing more distress than is necessary." Nancy wandered over to the washbowl and dipped her hands into the water. "Would you like me to stay with you, my lady?"

"Of course she wants you to stay. Are you forgetting I'm standing in her ladyship's bedchamber?" Mackenzie turned to Lillian. "I've done some investigating and Heather returned to her cottage after supper. Ursula left an hour ago."

"And Mary? I said she could go home to the cottage tonight to collect some of her things. That was just before supper. She promised to return tomorrow."

Mackenzie shuffled his feet and peered over his shoulder at Nancy Hill who was busy tidying the books. He turned back to Lillian and whispered, "Mary left a little later than you thought. W-we ate supper together, got to talking about the old days when she worked at her father's inn."

Lillian shivered as a cold chill swept through her. "What time did she leave?"

"An hour ago, but it couldn't have been Mary. As God is my witness, she'd never harm a soul."

Lillian's mind was a muddle. She wanted to trust Mackenzie's word. Mary didn't seem like a woman capable of violence. But then the men had trusted her husband, Doyle, before he betrayed them.

Oh, she wished Fabian were here. He would know what to do. He would handle the matter in the same masterful way he handled everything. Lillian caught herself. What had happened to her desire for independence and freedom? All she wanted was her husband home.

"Let us hope Lord Ravenscroft returns tomorrow." Lillian sighed inwardly. Leaving the island was no longer an option. With the master away, it was her responsibility to deal with any crisis. "In the meantime, we will continue as though nothing has happened. Should anyone ask, I fell and hit my head on the wooden chest. You will make discreet inquiries. I will converse with the women concerned and watch for any sign that might lead me to suspect them."

Mackenzie bowed. "And what of Mrs Hill?"

The housekeeper jumped at the mention of her name. "On my oath, I'll not utter a word to no one."

"Good," Mackenzie said, "as I doubt his lordship will allow the husband of a gossip to command his finest ship."

Nancy smiled through gritted teeth. "I'm a woman of my word, Malcolm Mackenzie. You know that."

"Aye, and a lot of foolish words they are to boot!"

Lillian raised her chin. "Strange things are afoot. I have taken you both into my confidence, and I expect you to behave accordingly." It was time to act like the wife of the infamous Raven and not some naive lady from the city, crippled by scandal and gossip.

Mackenzie cleared his throat. "I had arranged for the men to demonstrate their parrying skills in a competition tomorrow. Shall I postpone the event until his lordship returns?"

"No." It was best they continue as planned. Besides, she needed a distraction, something to banish all thoughts of Vane and Fabian from her mind. "If we alter our plans it will seem as though we are living in fear." And by God, she'd spent enough time worrying, enough time being controlled by the will of others.

"Very well, my lady."

"I want guards posted on the gatehouse. No one is to enter or leave without permission. And I want a log kept of all movements from the castle to the dock."

A smile touched the corners of Mackenzie's lips. The gleam in his eyes made him look like a proud parent. "I'll see to it at once, my lady. Now, we shall leave you to get some rest."

Mackenzie stepped back and gestured for Nancy to exit the room. The Scot was about to close the door when Lillian suddenly had an idea.

"Oh, Mackenzie, before you go."

"My lady?"

"Please add my name to the list of contestants eager to show their parrying skills." If she hoped to serve these men in Fabian's absence, she would need to gain their respect. "I should like to compete."

The man's eyes bulged and almost popped out of their sockets. "Compete?"

"Yes. You will find me a rapier and deliver it here first thing in the morning so I might practice."

A stunned silence ensued.

"But his lordship—"

"Has granted me the freedom to do as I please. And so I trust you will carry out my request."

"Of course, my lady," he said with some reluctance.

"Then I shall see you bright and early."

As Mackenzie closed the door, Lillian could no longer contain the surge of excitement. A contest was the perfect distraction. Equally, it was a way of proving she had the skill to kill a man, should anyone wish to challenge her again.

CHAPTER FOURTEEN

The shouts and jeers carried through the air for half a mile or more, the vigorous sound full of fire and aggression. The castle walls came into view. Fabian half expected to find men clambering over the ramparts, charging the doors with a battering ram or firing giant rocks from a catapult. But life outside the castle looked as peaceful as when he had left.

Fearing mutiny was afoot, Fabian broke into a run, leaving his men to trudge behind carrying Lillian's trunk. His need to hurry stemmed from more than a fear of whatever was going on beyond the wall. For the first time in his life, he had missed home.

Four days away felt like forever. Lord, he'd spent endless months at sea, and never experienced the odd sense of separation. Home happened to be wherever he bedded down for the night. Now, *home* came in the form of a raven-haired beauty with eyes that bewitched a man at first sight.

He reached the gatehouse only to find the wooden doors shut, and so banged hard with his fist in the hope someone could hear him through the din. Isaac appeared at the square peephole and peered through the bars.

"Are we expecting an invasion?" Fabian mocked, although

judging by the boisterous sounds coming from within, it sounded like a celebration.

"My lord, you're back." Isaac stepped away, raised the wooden barricade and opened the door. "Lady Ravenscroft wants to know who's coming and going. We're all to take turns guarding the door."

Panic flared.

"Has there been some sort of incident?" A host of images flooded his mind. Had Aubrey broken out of his prison cell? Did the man have an accomplice who'd crept into the castle at night to rescue him? Damnation. Perhaps he'd been wrong to leave Lillian for so long, although it couldn't be helped. After hearing Lillian's heartrending story, dealing with Lord Cornell had become a priority.

"Not that I know of, my lord. Her ladyship gave the order last night."

The order? Intrigued by his wife's ability to command his men in his absence, Fabian strode through the gate, eager to hear more.

"Has her ladyship given any other orders while I've been away?"

"She forced Mackenzie to open the dungeon so she could speak to the prisoner." Isaac shook his head and sighed. "Mackenzie tried his best to stop her, but it seems she had her mind made up."

An unusual mix of pride and anger filled his chest. He wanted to worship Lillian's strength and courage, wanted to take her by the arms and demand to know what the bloody hell she thought she was doing.

The clash of metal and another loud jeer drew his attention. "Please tell me the men aren't fighting. I know they suffer from bouts of boredom when not at sea but there are better ways to spend their time."

Isaac bit his bottom lip and struggled to hold Fabian's gaze. "They're fighting, my lord, with swords, but—"

"Swords!" Heaven help him. "And Mackenzie allowed such antics with my wife in residence?"

"Well ..." A weird groan escaped Isaac's lips. "Well ... you see, Lady Ravenscroft is a competitor."

Had Isaac punched Fabian on the nose, he would not have been more stunned. "Excuse me?"

Isaac shrank back. "There's a competition to test parrying skills. So far, Lady Ravenscroft has beaten every man who's stood against her."

Fear gripped him this time. One wrong swipe and the damn woman would be married and buried all in the same week.

Without further ado, he strode into the bailey and joined the crowd of men gathered around in a circle.

"Och, how I wish I had taken bets," Mackenzie cried. "I would be a rich man now that's for sure."

Fabian kept his head bowed as he joined the excited throng. Everyone was too busy watching his wife cross swords with Skinny Malinky to notice him.

"Remember, the winner of this bout is declared the champion." Mackenzie gave a hearty chuckle. "Sorry, Malinky, but you'll need your wits about you if you plan on beating her ladyship."

"Make no allowances for me." Lillian's sweet voice pierced the air.

Fabian's gaze drifted to his wife's flushed cheeks and beaming smile. His stomach lurched. The muscles in his abdomen grew tight, and he doubted he had ever seen a more welcoming sight.

Only when both opponents stepped back and raised their swords, did Fabian notice that his wife wore a gentleman's shirt, breeches and a pair of scuffed boots. Based on her unconventional attire, he'd expected to see her hair hanging loosely about her shoulders, but it was swept up into a chignon that worked in opposition to the rest of her attire.

Skinny struck out with his sword, the clang of metal drawing a gasp from the crowd. Fabian bit back a curse. To cry out would startle his wife and he could not take the risk of her making a mistake.

Lillian used a basic parry to defend the attack, a more complex "parry of four" to defend the blow to her right side. Impressive. Skinny dealt with her counterattack with skill and precision. The man's long legs made him light and nimble on his feet. Lillian was able to ward off the next strike and returned with three consecutive blows that left Skinny stumbling.

Pride replaced Fabian's apprehension. Lillian demonstrated remarkable swordsmanship. He watched in awe as she performed a move akin to a pirouette, twirling around until she ended up behind Skinny, the point of her rapier digging into his back.

Everyone cheered.

"The lady ain't no siren," one of his men muttered. "She's a warrior if ever I've seen one."

Mackenzie stepped forward, his chest puffed and his face aglow. "I'm sure you will all agree. Lady Ravenscroft is the winner of this competition."

The smile on Lillian's face warmed Fabian's heart. She deserved all the good things life had to offer: friendship, passion, love—and he would be the one to give them to her. After his trip to London, that bastard Cornell knew Fabian would bury him in a shallow grave as fodder for the body snatchers, should he do anything to harm the wife of the Raven.

"Indeed," Mackenzie continued, "our lady has beaten every man here."

"Not every man," Fabian shouted, weaving through the

spectators. He shrugged out of his coat and handed it to one of his men. "I believe I am yet to compete."

Gasps and excited whispers filled the air.

Lillian sucked in a breath. Her eyes widened though not from shock. Warmth radiated from those glistening gems. She looked ready to race into his arms, but she straightened her shoulders and a coy smile played on her lips.

"Are you sure you want your men to witness your defeat, my lord?"

Some of his men chuckled only to paste a serious expression when he glared into the crowd. "I mastered the art of swordsmanship while you were sewing with your threads."

She clenched her jaw and raised her chin. "I received expert tutorage from the Italian master Alvaro Romano."

"Did my men know that before you set them the challenge?"

"Of course not. Surely you know that the art of surprise plays to one's advantage."

Fabian smiled. Her confidence roused his desire. How was he to demonstrate his swordsmanship when he could think of nothing but thrusting into her sweet body?

"Oh, I have a few surprises that might make this a far more exciting challenge." Fabian gestured for Skinny to lend him the sword. Skinny obliged, and Fabian practised a few lunges, swung the sword around his head to loosen the muscles in his wrist. "But I anticipate it will be over in a matter of minutes."

"Over confidence is as debilitating as a chink in a knight's armour."

"Is it over confidence or merely an accurate interpretation of my skill?" God, he'd missed her company. He missed the witty banter, missed the challenging glint in her eyes. Seeing her now banished the dull ache in his chest, the constant reminder that life without her was unimaginable now. Fabian caught himself. He'd not just missed her these last few days—he'd missed her these last eight years.

They took their positions and touched swords. He waited for her to strike first and countered her attack. They teased each other, tapping swords, trying surprise lunges. Lillian swiped the air with her rapier, the whipping hiss a means to intimidate. What she lacked in strength, she made up for in the sheer grace of her movements.

They clashed swords. He deliberately locked his blade against hers in order to close the gap between them. "Have you missed me, Lilly?"

"Perhaps I should ask you the same question. You've been gone for four days."

"From your tone, I detect the answer is yes."

They stood rigidly, their swords crossed. The sharp blades were the only thing stopping him from kissing her. Using brute strength, he forced her sword to the left and stole a kiss.

The surprise move threw her off balance. The men jeered. Lillian's cheeks flushed a pretty shade of pink and she swung at him, frustration evident. Fabian blocked the hit and drew them together again.

"Are you determined to put me in an early grave?" Fabian gazed at her lips, eager to taste them, to part them with his tongue and delve deep inside. "I almost expired on the spot when I saw you fighting with Skinny."

She jerked her head, flicking away the lock of hair draped across her left eyebrow. "And I hardly slept a wink wondering where you were and what had happened to you."

"So you were worried about me." His smile faded when he noticed the cut above her brow. "What the hell happened to your eye?" Lord, he felt sick to his stomach. He was about to scold his men for their carelessness in combat, but the crusting around the wound confirmed it wasn't fresh.

"I had an accident." She knocked his sword aside, grabbed his waistcoat and kissed him roughly on the lips before stepping back and jabbing the rapier at him again.

Desire raged through his body. Anger fought to dampen his ardour. The internal war threw him off kilter. Fabian cursed himself for leaving her alone. And yet all thoughts turned to rousing a pleasurable sigh from her lips. Indeed, it took every ounce of concentration left to ward off Lillian's attack.

"Did you have to leave me on my wedding night?" she blurted, as her blade slashed the air.

"Would I have left had it not been necessary?" Hot blood raced through his veins. He raised his sword and defended her attack. "There is no place I'd rather be than in your arms."

Her mouth fell open, and her breath came in ragged pants. His comment proved too hard to defend. The sword slipped from her grasp.

Everyone gasped as they watched the outcome with eager anticipation.

"Is that the truth?" she whispered.

Fabian threw his sword to the ground. "You know I never lie."

With some hesitance, she moved towards him. He opened his arms to welcome her and she ran the last few steps, jumped into his embrace and kissed him.

Nothing tasted as good as her lips. Somehow, she had gained confidence in her ability whilst he'd been away. She was the one to draw her tongue across the seam of his lips. She was the one moaning into his mouth as their tongues tangled.

"Come on now. Can you not see the competition is over?" Mackenzie whispered. "Be gone, you rowdy rabble."

By rights, Fabian should tear his mouth away, carry his wife to their private chamber and continue what they had started. But he was held spellbound by the depth of her passion, held rigid by the powerful emotions filling his chest.

One man's mutterings reached his ears. "I know she threw her sword down first, but in my book, the lady is the winner."

Lillian broke contact. She stared into Fabian's eyes as she tried to catch her breath.

"Do you want to continue this somewhere else?" He had to ask. It wouldn't do to be presumptuous.

"You know I do."

"I've spent four days on the road. Perhaps a dip in a hot tub is advisable first."

Her hand came to rest on his chest. "I don't care about that." She pressed her lips to his again, this time the kiss was slow, heart-stoppingly sensual. Lillian spoke to his soul in a way no other woman ever had.

Fabian took her hand. "I have a better idea. One which will appease both of us." Without warning he scooped her up into his arms, relishing in her playful shrieks, in the closeness of her body as she threw her arms around his neck.

After a tiring few days, he wasn't sure how he found the strength to carry her up the stairs to their bedchamber. He barged the door open with his shoulder, trying not to drop her when she nuzzled his neck. With the heel of his booted foot, he kicked the door closed and delivered his wife to the comfort of the bed.

Lillian flopped back on top of the coverlet, her arms stretched above her head in wanton abandon. The loose-fitting shirt gave no indication as to the soft round breasts beneath. Still, he could imagine her nipples hardening under the heat of his gaze.

"Is there water in the bowl?" He resisted the urge to pull her shabby boots off, to tug down the breeches and settle between bare thighs.

She glanced at the washstand. "Yes, it's relatively clean if not a little cold."

"Good." He grabbed her hand and pulled her to her feet. "Find a linen cloth while I strip."

"And I suppose you want me to wash you as well," she teased.

Fabian raised a brow. "What, don't you want to rub your hands over my naked body?"

A blush touched her cheeks. She took a moment to reply. "When you put it like that perhaps I can be persuaded."

While she found a cloth and swished it about in the water, he undid his waistcoat and threw it onto the chair. His boots followed, and he unbuttoned his breeches and left them hanging on his hips.

Lillian wrung the water from the cloth and came to stand before him. "I'm surprised to see you wearing a cravat. I thought you'd wear less formal attire while on the road."

"I draw enough attention when seen in London," he said, unravelling the length of silk. "A lord without an elegant cravat is like a king without a crown."

"So you were in London?"

Although they were not clawing at each other in a rampant frenzy, the air thrummed with sexual tension. "I went to confront Lord Cornell and to bring you some clothes." He drew his shirt over his head and added it to the pile of discarded garments. To distract her would lessen the blow when he told her the news.

"Lord Cornell?" Lillian's heated gaze drifted over his chest. "What did you say to him?"

Fabian sucked in a breath as she drew the cold cloth across his shoulder and down his arm, rubbing the linen over his bicep. "It wasn't what I said but more what I did."

Lillian's hand stilled. "Please tell me you didn't meet him on the common at dawn."

"I only duel with gentlemen. I consider Cornell to be vermin."

Lillian continued to wipe his chest and abdomen with the linen square, each time moving closer to the band of his breeches. "So what did you do?"

"We kidnapped him as he left his club, stripped him naked

and chained him to railings in Portman Square." Fabian had come close to driving a blade through the cold bastard's heart.

"Good Lord!" Her eyes widened. "Can you not hang for committing such a crime?"

He bent his head and kissed the frown from her brow. "There were no witnesses. The man was terrified out of his wits. I returned at dawn and released him on the proviso he refrain from all attempts to persecute you or your brother."

"And you can trust his word?"

"He knows I will kill him if he hurts you again. I intend to send him a raven feather once a week as a stark reminder." He smiled. "I think you need to rinse the cloth and begin again."

"I told you, I don't care about a bit of dust." Her breath came quickly. "A man should smell of the road and leather, not fancy soap and perfume."

Fabian pushed his breeches off his hips. His hard cock sprang free. "Perhaps you could attend to one more task before you discard the linen."

After a brief hesitation, she wrapped nervous fingers around his shaft. "It would be my pleasure." With care, she wiped the cloth over the length of him. "Did you ask Cornell about his connection to Lord Martin?"

Fabian struggled to think as she cleaned and massaged him. "Revenge is his motive. Lady Cornell believes she's in love with your brother and … oh, that feels so good."

"It is as I suspected then."

"Indeed. But you never need think of it again. You're free."

"And that was your reason for leaving me?" Both hands gripped his cock now. She eased slowly back and forth until all rational thoughts left him.

"I'll not have you living in fear. By now—" A groan left his lips. "You must know I would do anything for you." He closed his eyes and relished the sensation of warm fingers gliding up and down in a sweet rhythm. "Now, perhaps you should remove your clothes, so I may see what I've missed these last few days."

"Four days," she corrected. She stood before him and stripped slowly, purely as a means to torment him for his long absence.

Fabian wrapped his arms around her waist and pulled her to his chest. "Tell me you want me, Lilly. Tell me I'm forgiven for bringing you here."

Her eyes brimmed with emotion, and she smiled. "I want you more than I've wanted anything my entire life. And I want to thank you for bringing me here."

She twined her arms around his neck and kissed him deeply. He loved the feel of her soft mouth. He loved the way her pliant body moved so sensually against his. Most of all he loved … he loved her.

CHAPTER FIFTEEN

The warm water soothed Fabian's tired bones. Draping his legs over the end of the copper tub, he immersed his head and shoulders. It had crossed his mind to have his wife wash him again this morning. But they'd spent the night becoming better acquainted. He'd explored every uncharted inch of her body, discovered every sensitive spot, mapped a perfect route to the exotic island of pleasure.

He closed his eyes as the water hummed in his ears like the sea's heartbeat. Ordinarily, the relaxing rhythm calmed him and drowned out all fearful thoughts of Estelle, morbid thoughts that pushed to the fore during moments of solitude. But a soul-deep contentment filled his chest. One attributed to the beautiful woman asleep in his bed. If marriage to the woman he'd thought lost to him was possible, so was the prospect of finding Estelle.

A dark shadow passed over his closed lids. It moved back and forth before hovering overhead. A light breeze tickled his cheek, and his heart skipped a beat as he pictured Lillian standing over him, gazing upon his naked body.

Fabian opened his eyes slowly, eager to savour the sight of her full lips and mussed hair. Perhaps he might catch her peeking in places she dared not look. But unless his wife had grown in a thick red beard during the night, something was dreadfully wrong with his imagined scene.

"Good God, Mackenzie," Fabian whispered through gritted teeth, his face mere inches from the Scot. He sat up, forcing Mackenzie to straighten.

"Och, praise be. I thought you were dead."

"Keep your voice down else you'll wake Lady Ravenscroft." Fabian glanced at the closed curtains on the four-poster bed. "Is there something wrong?"

Mackenzie raised the bucket in his hand. "You asked for more hot water, my lord."

"So I did. Leave it here, and I shall see to it myself."

Mackenzie nodded and placed the bucket on the floor. With a grimace, he tiptoed backwards as though it made his clunky steps quieter.

No sooner had the door closed than the curtains twitched. Lillian poked her head out between the green velvet panels. "So, you're a man who enjoys an early morning soak?"

Early morning? It was almost twelve. "I'm a man who enjoys many of life's pleasures."

"Did I not do a thorough job last night?"

Fabian couldn't stop a grin forming. "The answer depends upon whether we're talking about bathing."

"What else would we be talking about?" Her tone held a seductive lilt.

"I couldn't possibly say." He swished the water over his chest just to tease her. "But I am in need of your expert assistance."

Lillian raised a coy brow. "What, now?"

"The water's cold and needs heating up."

One slim ankle appeared through the gap in the curtain, followed by a soft creamy-white thigh. Her gaze darted nervously from the tub to the door.

"I suggest you lock it. Mackenzie often forgets to knock."

Baring her naked body bit by bit, she eventually padded over to the door and turned the key. Fabian rested his head against the rim of the tub, entranced by the sight of her round buttocks.

Holding her arms awkwardly across her stomach and chest, she came to stand before him. "Would you like me to pour warm water over your back, my lord?" A shiver shook her body, and her teeth chattered.

"What I'd like is for you to get into the tub with me."

Her eyes grew wide as she scanned the length of his body. "There's barely enough room for you in there."

"Trust me. I shall make room. Pirates are renowned for being resourceful."

"You're not a pirate."

"I am now," he said, offering a wolfish grin. He sat up straight and pressed his back against the tub. "I intend to plunder your mouth and take your precious bounty."

Without further protest, Lillian stepped in and lowered herself down. She was right. There wasn't any room, and she had to sit on his lap. Not that he had any complaint.

"Lie back against my shoulder." Fabian eased her gently back, swished water over her stomach and breasts until she relaxed.

A chuckle escaped her lips.

"What is it?"

"For a moment, I imagined myself back at Sandford Hall, seeing Francis' face as she appeared behind the screen to offer me my robe. My maid would swoon if she saw me like this."

Fabian took her hand and pressed her palm against his. "As I told you the night you arrived. Here, you're free to be yourself. With me, you need never censor your words or actions."

The more time he spent with her, the more he glimpsed the fun-loving young woman he remembered. And yet, he liked the inner strength she possessed now, the strength that gave her the courage to blow a blade from a man's hand and wield a sword like a warrior.

"On the subject of maids," he continued, threading his fingers with hers. "The one in Berkeley Square gave me a handful of dresses and undergarments. The trunk should be in your bedchamber, along with the pistols you requested and a small blade in a sheath."

As expected, Lillian tried to turn around to face him but could only glance up over her right shoulder. "You saw Vane?" Panic infused her tone. "Why did you not mention it before?"

"We have been somewhat preoccupied since my return. Besides, Vane was out. Bamfield granted me entrance although I did not give the butler much choice in the matter."

Fabian had hoped to apprise Vane of the situation before he came to the island. Yes, they would have fought. But it would have spared Lillian any more heartache.

"I waited for three hours, went to his club, visited the usual haunts. In the end, I had no choice but to write a letter."

"Wh-what did you say?" Her body trembled against his.

"Nothing other than where he might find you. I left directions for him to come to Branscombe. The fishermen there know to ferry Vane across if need be."

Vane had visited the Eight Bells, almost throttled the landlord in a bid for information, although Jim told him nothing.

"Did you mention our marriage?"

"No. I thought it best we deliver the news in person."

"I see."

"All will be well. I promise you that." He had every confidence Vane would come to accept the situation. But in the interim, it wouldn't be pretty. "Come, the water is cold. Let's climb back into bed, and you can tell me what you've been doing in my absence."

In an effort to stand, she came up on her knees and gripped

the end of the tub for balance. The sight of her lush, round buttocks inflamed his desire.

"On second thoughts, stay exactly where you are." Fabian came up on his knees behind her.

"Why, are you struggling to get out?"

"We're not getting out just yet."

He grabbed the bucket and emptied the hot water into the bath tub. Cupping his hands, he trickled the water over her back. He found the cake of soap and washed her, massaging the muscles in a slow seductive rhythm until her shoulders relaxed.

"What would your maid think if she could see you now?" he drawled as he reached around and fondled her breasts.

Lillian arched her back, pressing her buttocks against his already engorged cock. "She would swoon on the ... hmm ... on the spot."

He gripped her hip with his left hand while his right hand stroked a sweet rhythm between her thighs. "Tell me you want me." Regardless how many times he'd taken his wife, after her harrowing experiences in the past he would always seek permission.

"I want you, Fabian." Her breath came in ragged pants. Soon her climax would be upon her, and he wanted to be inside her when she came apart. "I want you now."

Needing no further inducement, he entered her in one long fluid movement until buried to the hilt. Good God, she felt divine. In her quest for satisfaction, she rocked back and forth, slapping against him, hugging him tightly.

"Hurry, Fabian." Her movements grew wild, urgent. Water splashed onto the floor.

This was different to the slow, tender lovemaking they'd shared hours earlier. This was about lust, about being free to express one's passion without thought or censure.

"Come for me, love," he breathed as he pounded hard and

deep. Each thrust brought him closer to the blissful edge, too. "Let me hear you cry out. Let me see you soar on the dizzying heights of your release."

She shuddered against him, her thighs shaking.

"Let me hear you, love," he whispered. "Tell me how it feels."

"Oh, Fabian. It feels so good."

His groan of satisfaction reverberated in his chest as her words of praise drew his release from him. He stilled. Amid the intense burst of pleasure came a moment of pure clarity: a peace that he had never known, an overwhelming sense that everything in the world was right.

The distant rumble of thunder reached Fabian's ears as he lay sprawled and exhausted on his back in bed. Lillian's luscious leg was draped across his thigh as she drifted in and out of sleep. He waited for the moment of calm to best gauge the distance and ferocity of the storm—but it didn't come.

Somewhere, doors slammed with hurricane force. Groans and curses rained down in torrents. The thunderous growls moved ever closer. Only a fool would think that the loud crack ripping through the air was lightning.

Bloody hell!

Vane had wasted no time chasing after his quarry. Nor had he knocked the door politely and asked to see the master.

Fabian tried to move without disturbing Lillian, but the commotion continued outside the bedchamber door.

"Is this his room?" Vane's commanding voice was unmistakable.

"God's teeth, you can't go in there," Mackenzie protested. "Let me wake them first—"

"Them! Move out of my way, Scot. I'll not tell you again."

Lillian stirred. She yawned and rubbed her eyes. With mussed hair and swollen lips, she looked as though she truly had been ravished by a pirate.

A thud preceded a splintering snap as the door burst open.

Lillian gasped in shock, but Fabian pressed his finger to her lips.

"I would resist tugging the curtains if I were you." Fabian grabbed the edge of the sheet and pulled it up to cover Lillian's modesty. Although he couldn't see Vane, the tension in the air was like a lead weight pressing down on them. "Wait downstairs, and I'll meet you there once I'm dressed."

As soon as he heard the growl of disapproval from beyond the curtain, Fabian knew he'd been careless with his choice of words.

"Get out of there now, before I drag you out." The material suddenly ballooned in the middle as Vane hit out in temper. "I swear I shall hang you from a gibbet and watch while the crows peck at your rotting flesh."

"He's got a pair of duelling pistols, my lord," Mackenzie shouted. "Make no sudden movements."

"Please, Vane," Lillian cried, gripping Fabian's forearm. "I beg you. If you care for me at all wait downstairs, and I shall explain everything."

"Lillian?" Panic and relief clung to that one word.

A heavy silence ensued.

Fabian's racing heartbeat filled his ears. This was what he'd been waiting for: a chance to confront Vane, the opportunity to get him on a side. He sensed Vane retreat before he heard the clip of booted footsteps on the stone floor.

Mackenzie must have trailed after the lord, for when Fabian peered through the gap in the curtain the room was empty.

They set about dressing quickly. Neither spoke. The stillness belied the internal roar of minds bombarded by questions, of a growing unease that made their limbs work clumsily.

Once ready, Lillian stopped and stared at him. From her ashen face and rapid blinking, he knew fear filled her heart. He stepped towards her and drew her into an embrace.

"Vane's anger will abate once he hears my story, once he sees that you're happy here." He cupped her cheeks and kissed her tenderly on the mouth. "You are happy?"

"Ecstatically so." She glanced briefly at the floor. "But I cannot bear to see hurt and disappointment in his eyes, Fabian."

"It will pass. Tomorrow we will look upon a bright sky absent of clouds, but for now, we must ride the storm."

Lillian nodded weakly. "Then let us go and find him. Patience is not a trait Vane has mastered."

With a firm grip of Lillian's hand, Fabian led her downstairs. Some of his men were standing in the corridor outside the great hall. They shuffled back sheepishly upon his approach.

"The man has pistols, m'lord, and he ain't afraid to use them."

"Return to your work," Fabian said with an air of confidence. "It is nothing I cannot handle." Fabian opened the old oak door and gestured for Lillian to enter. "Regardless what you hear, you're to remain outside."

Mackenzie sat on the bench, watching Vane pace the floor in front of the dais. Both pistols lay on the table. Dressed in black, the man had the menacing aura of the Devil. Vane turned to face them. Were it not for his glacial stare, Fabian could have believed the lord had risen from the fiery pits of Hell.

Mackenzie came to his feet. "I'd give Trevane a wide berth. The man is madder than a wet hen."

Lillian ignored Mackenzie's advice and rushed forward. "Vane! I'm so glad to see you."

Her brother embraced her, stroked a hand down her loose hair and examined her face. He took hold of her chin and tilted her head to better study the cut above her eye.

Fabian groaned inwardly.

Vane moved Lillian aside. "What the hell have you done to her?" Deciding not to wait for a reply, a guttural roar pierced the air and he charged forward.

Fabian braced himself for an attack. Vane had broader shoulders, was an inch or two taller, but had not spent years sailing the harsh seas.

Vane lunged and tried to take Fabian down to the floor but even in the lord's rage he struggled to unbalance the Raven.

"No man is steadier on his feet than me," Fabian mocked. The skill came from clinging to the rigging during high winds, from trying to steer a ship through turbulent waters.

With his jaw clenched so hard one could hear the grinding of teeth, Vane threw a punch that landed on Fabian's cheek and almost knocked his head off his shoulders. An uppercut to the ribs stole Fabian's breath.

Fabian stumbled, but as a participant in many brawls in the seedier ports dotted around the West Indies, he knew how to take a hit.

"Fight back, you damn coward."

"Stop this," Lillian cried.

By rights, Fabian deserved a beating. He would thrash Vane to within an inch of his life were the roles reversed. "Don't think I can't take you. I've fought fiercer men than you and lived to tell the tale," Fabian goaded him. The sooner Vane achieved satisfaction and his anger subsided, the sooner they could converse like mature, rational men.

Vane took the bait and charged at Fabian again, this time swiping his leg from underneath him while gripping him around the waist. They wrestled on the cold flagstones. Vane came above him and gripped his shirt.

"Go on." Fabian smirked. "You may hit me until your knuckles bleed but it won't change a damn thing."

Vane drew back his fist. "You arrogant bastard."

"No! Please, Vane." Lillian rushed forward and tried to step in between them. She tugged the sleeve of Vane's black coat. But when that proved futile, she dropped to her knees and threw her arm across Fabian's chest. "Don't hurt him."

Despite having received numerous punches, Fabian's heart swelled at her concern for his welfare.

Vane turned on her. "Good God! After what he's done to you, I should kill him."

"Why, when you have not even given him a chance to explain?"

"Explain! What the hell is there to say? He abducted you from Vauxhall, all because I wouldn't play the obedient lord and go on his pathetic ghost hunt."

Fabian's blood boiled. "Estelle is alive. Why won't you trust my word?"

Vane released Fabian's shirt and straightened. "Let us say for one ridiculous moment that you speak the truth, and in a desperate bid to save your sister you ruined mine. What I cannot fathom is why you thought such an idiotic plan would persuade me to help you?"

"I have not ruined your sister," Fabian snapped. "If anything, I have saved her from spending a life living in your shadow."

Deep lines appeared on Lillian's brow. "Don't fight."

"Och, can't you see you're upsetting the lass?" Mackenzie added.

Vane ignored them. "Oh, you think preying on a vulnerable woman is honourable. She has suffered enough." His glassy eyes resembled the surface of a frozen lake: a cold hard exterior that promised danger beneath its icy depths. "The last thing she needed was to be a pawn in your game."

With Lillian's assistance, Fabian came to his feet. "This is not a game. An innocent young woman is out there as we speak." He stabbed his finger at the door. "And you have the gall to suggest I find it an amusing way to pass the time."

Vane raised an arrogant brow. "Innocent? Is that what you believe? Trust me. Estelle knew what she was doing. I suppose whatever you were doing with my sister behind the bed hangings falls into your misguided definition of innocent, too."

"I'm misguided?" Fabian clenched his jaw. "I'm not the cold-hearted bastard who offered marriage and reneged."

Lillian sucked in a breath. "Fabian, please. Let us all sit down and discuss this in a proper manner."

"Proper?" Vane chided. "Ravenscroft knows nothing about integrity or decency." Vane stared down his nose at Fabian. "Find a pistol. I shall wait for you outside the castle walls. Pack your things, Lillian. We are going home."

"No!" Lillian rushed to her brother's side, grabbed his arm and shook it repeatedly. "Stop this, Vane."

"This pirate has treated you with nothing but disrespect. I will have satisfaction on your behalf." Vane seemed confident of success. "Now gather your belongings."

"Don't underestimate my skill in combat. And Lillian is not going anywhere." Fabian was about to break the news of their recent nuptials.

"I can't go with you," Lillian blurted. Her pained expression was like a knife to Fabian's heart. "I can't go with you because … because Fabian is my husband. This is my home now."

A deathly silence ensued.

Vane's eyes bulged. He opened his mouth but said nothing.

Mackenzie sidled towards the door. "I'll be outside should anyone need me."

"As her husband, it falls to me to protect her." Fabian could see Vane was struggling to absorb the news. "Lillian is my responsibility."

Vane shook his head. He turned to Lillian. "You married without telling me?"

"Under the circumstances, I had little option."

"You mean to tell me you married this heathen because he forced you?"

"No!" Lillian's frantic gaze shot back and forth between them both. "I wanted to marry him. We were good friends once. More than friends now."

The comment should have given Fabian hope for the future. Indeed it did. But he needed more than a mild expression of affection—he needed her love. A burning passionate love that poets professed was possible. The love Aristotle described as one soul occupying two bodies.

Vane shrank back. "And at no time before reciting your vows did you think to inform me?"

"There was no time. Please, Vane," Lillian implored. "What if Fabian is right? What if Estelle is alive? After what Father did, surely you owe it to them to offer your assistance."

"A man is not responsible for the sins of his parents," Vane countered. "Besides, Estelle chose her fate when she boarded *The Torrens* with another gentleman."

It took Fabian a few seconds for the words to penetrate his addled brain. "What the hell do you mean? Don't shift the blame. Everyone knows Estelle worshipped you."

"Perhaps none of us are fully apprised of the facts."

"Then surely it makes sense to find Estelle and put an end to the mystery," Lillian said with some frustration.

Vane's lip curled up in disdain. "Husband or not, I'll not help the man who used you so callously."

Lillian groaned. "Oh, we are going around in circles." She threw her hands in the air in resignation. "Come and find me once you have settled this matter like gentlemen. Only then can we sit down and decide what to do about Estelle." With that, she turned on her heels and strode from the room.

Fabian contemplated asking her to stay. But some things were best said far from a lady's ears. He waited until Lillian closed the door before speaking again. "What will it be? Shall we roll up our shirtsleeves and wrestle until one of us is the victor?"

"We both know who that will be."

"I've gained experience since we last partook in a little gentlemanly sport."

"Experience counts for nothing when a man has a grudge to settle." Fire flashed in Vane's eyes. Inside, he was hurting. Anyone could see that. Whether it stemmed from his guilt over Lillian, or Estelle, remained to be seen.

"Then you should know that I blame you for Estelle leaving." The pain in Fabian's heart had been eased by his growing feelings for Lillian. Still, Vane needed to have his anger beaten out of him if they had any hope of moving forward. "Eight years is a long time to hold a grudge." Fabian dragged his shirt over his head. "I vowed to make you pay for the part you played, and the Raven never breaks a promise."

CHAPTER SIXTEEN

The group of men standing huddled around the door jumped back as Lillian exited the great hall. Mackenzie stood with them, his anxious face showing concern for the welfare of his master.

"Why is it men act like children when they have a point to prove?" Lillian observed the men's blank expressions. Why would they understand? They often fought over the last piece of chicken.

"Come on now, move yourselves." Mackenzie shooed the men out into the bailey. "The work won't get done if we're all standing here gaping." Mackenzie returned to her side. "Do I need to act as referee?"

"No. Give them an hour to settle their grievances in their own way." Vane's reaction came as no surprise. She had expected him to bring the roof down. If anything, she was thankful he'd only thrown a few punches. "But I refuse to stand and watch them banter and brawl like schoolboys."

"It's clear Trevane has your best interests at heart, and his lordship will do anything to ensure your happiness."

A smile touched Lillian's lips despite the loud roar emanating from the ancient room. "You have faith in your master. He is lucky to have such a true and loyal friend."

The Scot's cheeks turned as red as his beard. "You know how to make a grown man blush, lass. But happen I don't deserve your good grace."

Lillian put her hand on Mackenzie's arm. "Do you say that because of what happened at Vauxhall?" Some might say she was far too forgiving, but at the time she'd been too weary to persecute the man for his mistakes. Now, she didn't see it as a mistake but a fated event beyond anyone's control.

A chorus of masculine curses reached her ears.

Mackenzie glanced at the studded oak door and tutted. "I know I should feel ashamed for taking you from your home, but I'd heard the way the master spoke of you. I knew his need to bring you here had as much to do with saving himself as it did Estelle."

The Scot knew what to say to placate her fears. "There was a time when I envisioned marrying Lord Ravenscroft. And now ..." Her mind conjured an image of the dark-haired pirate plundering her mouth. She had only to mention his name and her insides performed a series of somersaults. "Now, even after such a short time, marriage to the Raven is everything I hoped it would be."

Mackenzie covered her hand and gave it a gentle pat. "You should come with us on our next voyage. I can't see his lordship leaving you behind, and there's nothing like the sea air to invigorate the spirit."

While she had no love for long voyages, the thought of being squashed in a cabin with Fabian certainly had appeal. "Perhaps I could bring Mary with me as a companion. Would you like that, Mackenzie?"

"Happen I'd be tripping over my own feet with Mary aboard ship. How's a man to navigate the waters when his mind is away with the fairies?"

It suddenly occurred to her that she'd not seen Mary since the night of the attack. She had been so preoccupied with Fabian, one day had merged seamlessly into the next.

"Did you see Mary yesterday?" Lillian had seen Ursula. She'd asked the maid to style her hair despite taking part in the parrying competition. It had been a ploy, purely to gauge the woman's reaction after the incident with the intruder.

The corners of Mackenzie's mouth turned down. "I've not seen her since we shared supper. What with his lordship's return and watching the prisoner, I've not had a chance to visit her."

"I can go." She needed to divert her attention away from the two men fighting in the great hall. Hopefully, by the time she returned they would have put aside their differences. "The walk will do me good."

Mackenzie shook his head. "Och, don't trouble yourself, my lady. I'll find time to check on her today. Besides, after the attack in your chamber, his lordship won't want you going out alone."

Lillian forced a smile. Mackenzie assumed she'd told Fabian about the late-night intruder. She had planned to tell him but, like Vane, his need to protect her would prove stifling.

"Have you had any luck finding the treasure-hunting rabbits?" she said in a bid to change the subject. "Did you discover who has taken to digging up the heathland?"

Mackenzie glanced back over his shoulder before bowing his head. "I've not mentioned it to Lord Ravenscroft yet. After what happened with Doyle, I fear he'll distrust the men."

"Perhaps the culprit is merely looking for a way to occupy his time until his next voyage. I imagine most sailors long for a new adventure."

"Happen you're right. I've kept watch, but even the real rabbits are too shy to show themselves."

Mary had accompanied them on their inspection. Did she

know those responsible? Had she challenged them and now hid in her cottage in fear of her life?

"Let's hope they appear soon. I'm rather partial to Mrs Bell's rabbit stew."

"Aye, the woman knows—"

"There you are, Mackenzie." Mrs Bell waddled towards them bringing the smell of cooked apples with her. "Isaac said I'd find you here." Her mouth fell open when Mackenzie stepped aside and she spotted Lillian. Mrs Bell curtsied. "Forgive me for interrupting, my lady. What with Mackenzie's broad shoulders, I didn't see you standing there."

"That's quite all right, Mrs Bell. We were just discussing the merits of your rabbit stew."

The woman blushed. "Well, I can't take all the credit. My old mother's recipe never fails to hit the spot on a chilly night."

"You were looking for Mackenzie," Lillian prompted, ignoring the clatter from within the hall. "Please, do not let me stop you from your work."

"Oh, yes." Mrs Bell peered up at the man twice her height. "You asked me to tell you should anything else go missing from the kitchen."

Mackenzie shifted nervously.

"Things are going missing from the kitchen?" Lillian said. No one had mentioned it before. Perhaps one of the men had taken advantage of her husband's absence. "Have you informed Lord Ravenscroft?"

Mrs Bell seemed surprised she'd asked. "Mackenzie told the master."

"His lordship asked me to investigate," Mackenzie replied. "But there's been so much happening of late I've not got around to it."

Mrs Bell tutted. "It's food today but what might it be

tomorrow? Once a thief always a thief, that's what my old father used to say."

"Why would a man steal food?" With Fabian's wealth, surely he could afford to feed a thousand men.

"That's what I came to say." Mrs Bell reached into her apron pocket and removed a small metal object. "It's not a man were looking for. I found this in the pantry." She opened her fingers to reveal a cloak pin crafted in the shape of a thistle.

Mackenzie sucked in a sharp breath as his face grew pale.

"I might be wrong," Mrs Bell continued, "but does this not belong to Mary?"

Mackenzie paused before finally nodding. "Aye, that's Mary's pin. It belonged to her grandmother. The woman came from Skye hence the design."

"Well, I can't see she had cause to be in the pantry," Mrs Bell said. "Unless she was fetching something for you, my lady."

Once the gossip mill rolled, it wouldn't stop regardless of a person's innocence or guilt. And while Lillian had every reason to doubt Mary's loyalty, the distress marring Mackenzie's usually jolly countenance forced her to lie.

"I've struggled to sleep while here. I sent Mary down to the pantry two nights ago. Perhaps she dropped it then."

A flash of relief brightened Mackenzie's face, one quickly replaced by doubt. The man was no fool. He took a matter of seconds to recall that Mary had left the castle after taking supper with him.

Lillian straightened her shoulders and took the pin from Mrs Bell's hand. "I shall return this to Mary. In the meantime, I will assist Mackenzie in his search for the thief."

"Thank you, my lady." Mrs Bell clutched the ends of her apron and dipped a curtsy. "I'd best get back to my work."

No sooner had the woman turned the corner than Mackenzie released a weary sigh. "My lady, I cannot thank you enough for defending Mary. One word about this and the men would bundle her into a rowboat and leave her to the tide."

"You should have told me about the thefts." What with some men digging for treasure and others helping themselves to the contents of the pantry, Lillian was beginning to doubt the men's loyalty.

"Aye."

"While Lord Ravenscroft and my brother are solving their dispute, we shall visit Mary."

The fact the woman hadn't returned to the castle since the attack in Fabian's bedchamber, proved telling. And it was best Mackenzie was not alone when learning of Mary's duplicity.

"Wait here while I dress," Lillian continued. With her unkempt appearance, she looked more like a tavern wench than an aristocratic lady. "I shall be five minutes."

Mackenzie squirmed. "Begging your pardon, my lady, but I sent Ursula to the dock on an errand. The staff here have various roles, and I didn't think you'd be in need of her services this afternoon."

Things at the castle were certainly different from the rigid rules in London households, though Lillian found she much preferred the simpler way of life. "Pay it no mind. I think I am more than capable of brushing my hair and tying my cloak."

Mackenzie bowed. "Still, it was wrong of me not to consult you."

"We are all trying to adjust to our new circumstances. Wait for me here."

Lillian hurried to Fabian's room. One glimpse at the drawn hangings evoked memories of their wild adventure beneath the sheets. She tidied her clothes and found sturdy shoes in the trunk. After quickly plaiting her hair so it draped in true medieval style over one shoulder, she rushed downstairs to meet Mackenzie.

She passed the Scot in the corridor.

"Forgive me for not waiting, my lady. His lordship has asked for a bottle of brandy and two glasses, some warm water and squares of linen."

Lillian resisted the urge to throw her arms in the air and cheer. If they were drinking brandy, they were talking. She contemplated joining them but feared her presence might fuel the dying embers of her brother's rage.

"Then I shall wait for you in the bailey."

Mackenzie nodded and hurried away.

Lillian must have waited twenty minutes for Mackenzie though it felt like hours. He popped out into the bailey, raised his hand and informed her that he was to explain the events at Vauxhall to her brother. He apologised and said he would join her promptly.

Impatience got the better of her. It was only a matter of time before Fabian and Vane asked to see her. Perhaps she should make herself unavailable, merely to make a point. Indeed, tired of waiting for Mackenzie, she decided to visit Mary alone. The Scot knew where she was heading and could meet her at the cottages once he'd finished running errands.

Lillian was about to leave through the gatehouse when she met Ursula, carrying a wicker basket.

"My lady," Ursula said with some surprise. "I've just come from the dock. A few of the men are fishing and Mackenzie sent me to bring some back for Mrs Bell." Ursula peeled back the linen cloth to reveal their shiny silver scales.

"I'm sure Mrs Bell will be grateful." To reach the dock, Ursula had to venture past the cottages. "Did you see Mary on your travels?"

"No, my lady, I've not seen her of late." Ursula bit down on her bottom lip and her pale skin flushed pink. "I know you chose her to act as your maid and companion, and I don't mean to sound unkind, but the men don't trust her. After what Doyle did, I can't see that they'll ever accept seeing her here at the castle."

Sailors were a stubborn lot. Then again, perhaps Mary was as devious as her husband and sought to cause mischief at every opportunity. In the past, Lillian had been far too trusting and so refused to play the gullible fool again. There was only one way to discover the truth.

"Clearly, Mary is uncomfortable here as she's not been back for two days. Do the women feel the same way about her as the men?"

"It wouldn't have been too bad had Mary acted differently in the beginning. She swore she knew nothing of her husband's plans and yet she stayed away, hiding in her cottage, never seeing anyone."

"And you think that is an admission of guilt?"

Ursula shrugged. "I don't know what to think, my lady. But I find it strange that she stayed on the island when she has family in Truro."

A scandal of any sort often claimed innocent victims. It tarnished a family's reputation merely by association. Lillian understood why Mary kept away. She, too, had walked into a room only to have people stare and smirk. Some gave her the cut direct, eager to show their disdain. Cowards chose the indirect approach, pretending they'd not seen her to avoid any awkwardness.

"Has anyone spoken to Mary?" Lillian asked. "Has anyone questioned her about why she behaves as she does?"

"Most have made up their minds for themselves. They'd have put her in a rowboat back to the mainland, but his lordship refused to remove Mary from her home." A look passed over the wench's face when she referred to Fabian, one of admiration.

"Well, I'm on my way to visit Mary now. I shall speak to her and see what explanation she offers for her absence these last two days." There were but a few excuses the woman could use. Most telling would be her reaction when Lillian mentioned the injury she sustained in the bedchamber tussle.

Ursula frowned. "You shouldn't go alone, my lady." Her gaze drifted to the cut above Lillian's eyebrow. "After your nasty fall, you might still be unsteady on your feet. Wait while I take the basket inside and I'll come with you."

"Mackenzie is to accompany me when he's finished with Lord Ravenscroft." Knowing Fabian and Vane, they'd probably encouraged the Scot to drink with them. "As the wind has eased, and the sun is shining, I thought I'd take a leisurely stroll to the dock."

"Isaac said we're due a mighty downpour. I shall give the basket to Mrs Bell and keep you company until Mackenzie arrives." Ursula pursed her lips and sighed. "I'm not saying I don't trust Mary, but they say a sailor has the foresight of a gull for predicting storms. They sense something is wrong."

Since the scuffle with the intruder, Lillian had spoken to all the women of the same height and build—all except Mary. Heather and Ursula showed no sign of guilt. Just like the incident with Lord Martin, was someone else manipulating events to suit their purpose? And if so why?

"Speak to Mackenzie and tell him I am heading to the cottages. If he's occupied, then by all means, you may keep me company on the journey. But know that I intend to speak to Mary alone." If intimidation was the problem, then Mary would say nothing in front of Ursula.

Ursula smiled. "Have no fear, my lady. You can trust me."

CHAPTER SEVENTEEN

The wind whipped strands of hair loose from Lillian's plait as she stood on the cliff edge watching the waves crash violently on the rocks below. It was as if a sudden surge of energy had stirred the temperate waters into a frenzy. The temperature plummeted. Quick-moving clouds covered the clear sky, turning dark and threatening, eager to unleash an angry torrent on the world below.

Absorbed in the show of pure force, she failed to hear the approaching footsteps until Ursula tapped her on the arm. Swinging around in shock, Lillian stumbled back. The chalky earth crumbled beneath her feet. Ursula grabbed Lillian's cloak and pulled her away from the edge.

"Good Lord!" Lillian clutched her chest, her heartbeat pumping hard against her palm. "You frightened me half to death."

"I'm sorry, my lady, I thought you'd seen me coming along the path."

"When one stares out at sea it's easy to forget everything else exists."

"Sometimes, sailors look at it for so long they imagine green fields instead of murky water. Many a man has plunged to his death when he all he wanted was to feel land beneath his feet."

"When a man has a loving wife waiting at home, I imagine the months away can become tiresome." Lillian considered the woman standing before her. Ursula had hair the colour of spun gold. The ladies of the *ton* paid wigmakers a small fortune for hair half as vibrant. "Are you not inclined to marry?"

"Oh, I did marry. The drunken fool stumbled into the road on his way home, and a carriage mowed him down." An odd look passed over her face: relief, not grief. "Maybe I shall marry again one day. But I'm looking for a man with more about him."

"Do you mean intelligence?" In that regard, Lillian counted herself lucky. Many lords had nothing but sawdust between their ears, or a brain pickled by an excessive consumption of brandy. Fabian was well-read, had ventured to lands far and wide, could converse for hours on the merits of Plato over Aristotle.

"Intelligence?" Ursula scoffed. "Forgive me, my lady, but I was talking about money."

They both chuckled.

"When it comes to society marriages, money is all that matters." And an unblemished reputation, of course. Still, wealth was an attribute both sexes admired. Lillian had heard many ladies say that money could render an ugly man handsome.

"The same applies to common folk, too."

A biting chill in the air forced Lillian to gather her cloak across her chest. "Come. We should be on our way. With the impending storm, it's unwise to linger."

They strode in companionable silence along the clifftop path, towards the cluster of stone cottages in the distance.

"Did Mackenzie say he would join us?"

"His lordship sent him to ask Nancy to make a poultice to apply to your brother's knuckles. I think he meant to hit his lordship's cheek but punched the table instead."

Lillian groaned inwardly. What would the world come to if everyone thought to solve their problems with their fists, or to mask their fear and pain by throwing insults and punches?

"No doubt we'll be back before Mackenzie finishes running his lordship's errands." It suddenly occurred to her that she did not know where Mary lived. "If you direct me to the cottage you can wait here."

"I'll come as far as the well and wait for you there."

Ursula led Lillian to a row of terraced cottages. They were small. Each had a weather-beaten door and one tiny window. The grey mudstone gave them a cold, rustic feel, made drearier now black clouds obscured the sun.

"It's the one with the green door." Ursula pointed to the middle of the row. "Take as long as you need, my lady, and I'll keep you company on the way back. When the weather turns, it's best not to wander about alone."

"Thank you, Ursula."

The lane was deserted. Some of the men worked at the dock when not at sea. Some worked up at the castle, tending to the crops and livestock. As soon as Lillian knocked the door she knew something was wrong. The door creaked open though she heard nothing but an eerie silence within.

Lillian hesitated. Perhaps Mary had taken ill, and the poor woman's body lay cold and lifeless on the bed. She glanced over her shoulder at Ursula who immediately sensed something was amiss and came running.

"What is it, my lady?"

"The door was open."

Ursula peered through the narrow gap into the parlour-come-kitchen. "Most of us leave our doors open. We're like a family, forever popping in to share supper or to borrow cheese and bread."

The explanation sounded logical, were they not talking about

Mary. "Who amongst you would want to visit Mary? You said so yourself, no one trusts her."

Ursula nodded. "Maybe she's gone out, and this fierce wind blew the door. Probably best we return to the castle. The heavens are about to unleash a week's worth of rain by the look of it."

A sudden bang from inside the cottage made Lillian gasp. "Did you hear that?"

"As I said, my lady, it's probably the wind. Do you want me to see if Mary's left a window open?"

The patter of footsteps drew their attention. Lillian pressed her finger to her lips before pushing the door. They crept inside and followed the sound to the only other room in the house.

A figure appeared in the doorway.

Lillian's heart flew up to her throat.

"Heather?" Ursula said. "What are you doing here? Is this not Mary's cottage?"

A blush touched Heather's ashen face. "My lady! I noticed the door was open as I passed." Did the tremor in her voice speak of guilt or nerves? "After the rumpus yesterday, I thought it odd."

"Rumpus?" Ursula and Lillian said in unison as they exchanged curious glances.

"I heard raised voices. It went on for almost half an hour and then it went quiet."

"Did you not think to knock and enquire after her wellbeing?" Lillian asked. Perhaps one of Fabian's men had cause to confront Mary. Perhaps she *had* stumbled upon him digging for treasure.

"Folk don't go poking their nose in where it's not welcome."

What she meant was she didn't want the men to think she had sided with a traitor's wife.

"Well, did you find anything amiss?"

"There's a silver candlestick on the bed." Heather glanced back over her shoulder. "You don't think she stole it from the castle?"

A candlestick? The blood drained from Lillian's face.

"Things have been difficult since her husband left," Ursula added.

Lillian knew better than to jump to conclusions. Things were not always as they appeared, but the evidence against Mary was mounting. For Mackenzie's sake, she wanted to believe it was all a terrible misunderstanding.

Heather sighed. "Well, Mary isn't here."

Many times since returning to London, Lillian had wished she could run away and start a new life, somewhere far from the spiteful sneers and knowing glances. "Perhaps she has left the island. Why stay when everyone believes she is dishonest?"

Ursula shook her head. "None of the men would ferry her to the mainland without his lordship's consent."

"Did someone not tell me that sailors are a suspicious lot? Does it not stand to reason the men want rid of her?"

"All of Mary's belongings are here in the cottage," Heather added. "When a woman has no husband to support her, why would she leave with just the clothes on her back? The candlestick alone would fetch enough to feed her for months."

The comment resonated with Lillian. She had disappeared from Vauxhall without a trace. From her experience, one ran away of their own volition, or someone took them against their will.

"Then we must question the men and search the island."

"If the men sense your distrust there could be a mutiny," Ursula said. "It's not my place to contradict you, my lady, but we should be certain she's not on the island before we go accusing the men."

Ursula was right. They should search the area, scour the coastline. Perhaps Mary had wandered too close to the crumbling cliff edge. Worse still, had the rumpus Heather spoke about driven Mary to abandon this life altogether?

"Shall I wait here, my lady?" Heather shuffled nervously. "If Mary returns it might save endless hours of searching."

"Very well." Should Mackenzie join them, Heather could inform him of their plans. "We shall go down to the dock and follow the coastline."

"Maybe we should just go back to the castle, my lady."

"We will, but it won't hurt to have a quick look around."

With Ursula in tow, Lillian left the cottage and followed the lane to the dirt track leading to the shore.

The dock consisted of a large timber warehouse, and a few old buildings made of the same slaty mudstone as the cottages. A high stone wall kept the rising tide from flooding the area. A group of men were busy working. One man sat splicing a line on the landing pier leading to the frigate that brought her to the island. One man climbed the rigging. A few more were hammering wood on the poop deck. They were all too engrossed in their work to notice two women sneaking past.

"We should check the buildings." Lillian pointed to the warehouse. The wooden door stood ajar. "Mary might have wandered in there." It was highly unlikely.

Ursula nodded. She moved stealthily as if trying not to draw the men's attention. Peering inside, they found nothing but crates and barrels stacked neatly against the wall.

Lillian sighed. "I doubt Mary had a reason to come in here."

They moved to the stone buildings and found them locked.

"Mackenzie and Lord Ravenscroft are the only ones with a key." Ursula glanced back over her shoulder. "We should go back and stroll along the clifftop. When Mackenzie arrives, he can unlock these doors. It's best he speaks to the men."

Fear flashed in Ursula's eyes. Did she think the men had something to do with Mary's disappearance? Overcome by a sudden sense of foreboding, Lillian thought it best to return with Fabian or Mackenzie.

"We'll walk along the shore for a while." Lillian gestured to the path leading down to the beach. The first drop of rain landed on her cheek, and she wiped it away with the back of her hand. "If there's no sign of her we will return to the castle."

"What about trying the path north?"

Lillian considered Ursula's suggestion. "It's too far out of our way. Mackenzie can round up the men and conduct a thorough search once the weather improves. We'll head south."

With some reluctance, Ursula followed, her anxious gaze moving from the dark clouds looming overhead to the dock disappearing into the distance.

The tide ebbed, though their feet still squelched in the wet sand. Soon one drop of rain became two and three. An angry roar from the heavens gave them pause, and Lillian considered turning back.

"It looks like it will be one almighty storm." Ursula did not hide her apprehension.

"If we keep walking where will it take us?" Lillian quickened her pace. The gathering wind roared in her ears, and she had to repeat the question as Ursula failed to reply.

"To ... to the castle."

"Then is it not better to continue on our way?" Lillian clutched the hood of her cloak as a gale-force wind threatened to tear the clothes off her back. Without warning the shower turned into a torrential downpour. The gulls swooped and darted. Visibility diminished in seconds.

"Quick, my lady, we should turn back."

"It's too late."

They blinked to keep the rain from their lashes, held their arms out in front of them to maintain their balance. They moved closer to the cliff-face, to the cluster of rocks littering the beach.

"We should keep moving," Ursula shouted.

"No. We'll take shelter here. I'll use my cloak to shield us until the storm passes."

The rocks were rough and jagged, in varying hues of grey, and covered in barnacles. Lillian rushed behind them and was about to untie her cloak when she saw the narrow entrance to a cave.

Relief coursed through her.

"Quick, Ursula, I've found shelter. Hurry!"

Ursula stood on the beach, frozen to the spot. Was she afraid of being buried beneath a landslide? Did she know of the cave but had an irrational fear of the dark?

Lillian clambered over the scattering of giant stones. The entrance was nothing but a black mouth leading to heaven knows where. A pang in her stomach caused her to hesitate. But the inclement weather forced her inside.

She waited for Ursula, but the smell of smoke drew her attention to the cavernous space behind. Someone was in the cave. Unable to see the orange glow of a fire, she placed her hands on the damp wall and shuffled deeper inside.

What if Mary had sought sanctuary?

What if she needed a place to hide from the men?

"Mary?" Lillian continued through the puddles of stagnant water. Surely the woman wouldn't take refuge in a cave that flooded during high tide. "Mary, are you in here?"

The smell of smoke grew stronger, and Lillian noticed the faint amber light warming the rock face. The crack and pop of burning wood reached her ears. She turned right into a recess, saw the black pot hanging from a tripod over the campfire. A figure lay curled up into a ball on the ground.

Lillian rushed over and crouched down. One look at the fiery red locks and she knew she'd found Mary.

"Mary, can you hear me?" Lillian gripped the woman's arm and shook her. "Wake up."

Mary stirred. She raised her head off the ground and peered at

Lillian through half-closed eyes. "Lady Ravenscroft? Is it really you?"

"Are you hurt?"

Confusion marred the woman's brow. She blinked rapidly and tried to sit up. "You shouldn't be in here," Mary whispered, fear evident in her tone. "Go. You must go quickly before he comes back. Find Lord Ravenscroft. Go now."

Only when Mary gestured to the cave mouth did Lillian notice the rope binding the woman's hands. "Who did this to you? Was it one of the men?"

"There's no time. You must leave."

"But I cannot abandon you here."

A firm hand gripped Lillian's shoulder. "There you are, my lady." Ursula's voice brought instant relief until Mary's eyes almost bulged from their sockets.

"Oh, Lord, no!" Mary cried. "Run, my lady. Leave now before it's too late."

"Ain't no one leaving here without my permission." A man's hoarse voice pierced the air. "Ain't no one doing anything unless I say so."

Lillian swung around but could see no one in the gloom. "Who's there? Show yourself." She grabbed Ursula's arm and drew her closer. "Who are you?"

A low chuckle echoed through the cavernous chamber. "Why don't you ask your maid? Ask the snake you've taken to your bosom."

Lillian's head shot to Mary. But when the woman met her gaze, she saw nothing but truth and honesty there. Instinct forced her to turn to Ursula. "You're the one who stole into my bedchamber. You're the one acting as a traitor's eyes and ears."

Ursula stepped back. Panic marred her pretty face. "It wasn't meant to be like this. We need to find the treasure that's all."

"Treasure!" Mary shook her head. "If the Spanish had left

anything here they would have returned to claim it years ago. Without a map, it would take months to search the island."

"There is a map," Ursula countered. "It's hidden somewhere in the castle."

Mary snorted. "Don't listen to her, my lady. Fools and dreamers, that's what they are. They've spent too much time listening to the drunks in Branscombe."

The thud of booted footsteps preceded the figure appearing from the dark tunnel opposite. This strange-looking man was not one of Fabian's crew. No one would fail to notice this rogue in a crowd. Even in the dim cave, his bald head shone like polished silver. Two bushy brows met in the middle to form a frown.

"Mary's right," he snapped. "I've men chasing my heels. I don't have time to waste." He stepped closer, and Mary shuffled back. "I always knew Ursula was my good luck charm, and now she's brought the answer to my prayers." He jerked his head at Ursula, and she hurried to his side like an obedient pet.

"What do we do now?" Ursula asked. "Is it not best we leave?"

"Why leave when you've brought me a bounty?"

Ursula grimaced. The maid had tried her utmost to deter Lillian from walking along this stretch of coastline. Clearly, she worked for this man but did so begrudgingly.

"No," he continued. "You'll go to the castle and deliver a message. Five hundred sovereigns and a rowboat will secure her ladyship's release. Tell his lordship to bring the goods north of the dock, near Blackfriars' cove, at nine. Before the high tide."

"What about me?" Ursula gulped. "You promised me money, enough to start a new life."

His thin lips curved down into a permanent scowl which made it impossible to read his reaction. "You'll get your reward. Have no fear." He grabbed Ursula around the waist and kissed her roughly on the mouth. "The money will pay our passage to Jamaica. From there, we'll buy a share in a plantation."

"And what about me?" Mary said. "Would you leave your wife alone and destitute and take up with a strumpet?"

Lillian suppressed a gasp. So this was Doyle.

"Why do you care? Everyone knows you carry a torch for Mackenzie."

"Maybe that's because he's the kindest, most honest man I know."

Lillian watched the exchange. Did Doyle really think Fabian and Vane would hand over the money and watch him sail away? Heaven help the blackguard should Mackenzie get his hands on him.

"And what if Lord Ravenscroft cannot pay?" Lillian had to ask. They were miles from the mainland, further still from a bank.

Doyle winked and tapped his nose. "The Raven keeps a stash of loot locked away in the castle."

"What if he won't pay?"

"Ursula says the man's mind turns to mush when you're around. Besides, what's five hundred sovereigns when he's worth a king's ransom?"

Pride flooded Lillian's chest. Hard work and determination had brought Fabian from the brink of bankruptcy to a position of comfort and wealth. Not that it mattered to her. She loved him regardless.

The thought caught her off guard—stole her breath. She loved him. She felt the truth of it deep in her bones but had no time to examine her feelings further.

Lillian straightened her shoulders. "And how do you propose to make the exchange."

"You'll come in the boat with us. Once we're a few hundred yards out to sea, you can swim to the shore."

"And what if I can't swim?" Vane had made sure she could swim a mile in her clothes.

"Then you'll drown." Doyle picked up a length of rope and came towards her. "Now, your ladyship, turn around so I can bind your hands. I wouldn't want to leave you free to scratch my eyes out."

"Had I a blade to hand, I would do a damn sight more than that."

Doyle chuckled. "Ursula said you were a feisty one." He spun her around and tied her hands behind her back. She could have kicked him and tried to run, but she would not get far. As Doyle turned her back to face him, his greedy eyes settled on her locket. "What's this?"

"Touch it at your peril." The words were hard and unforgiving, yet inside, fear sucked the air from her lungs.

"A lady of your worth could buy a hundred more." Doyle wrapped his thick, chubby fingers around the chain and tugged. The fine links snapped. The chain slipped from her neck. For a second, her heart stopped beating.

"Give it back to me. It is worthless to you." Lillian held back the tears.

"Worthless? Nothing is worthless to a man with an empty belly." Doyle shoved the locket into his trouser pocket, and Lillian knew she would not rest until the locket was back in her possession. "Now sit down and keep your mouth shut." Doyle pushed her to the ground next to Mary.

"I'm sorry, my lady," Mary whispered. "It's my fault. If only I'd kept to my own business instead of snooping around the heathland at night. But I wanted to help Mackenzie."

"You have done nothing wrong." Lillian shot daggers at the blackguard as he took Ursula aside and repeated the instructions. "But mark my words. They will both pay for what they've done."

CHAPTER EIGHTEEN

" $\mathbf{G}$ od damn it!" Vane dabbed the poultice on his swollen knuckles and winced. "What the hell has your housekeeper put in this? It smells like rotten intestines."

"It's a concoction of herbs and oats." Fabian bit back a chuckle. "We're to have the intestines for supper. Pirates believe they're a delicacy."

"Well, if anyone should know it is you."

Fabian poured two glasses of brandy. He pushed one across the wooden table to Vane, took the other and sat on the bench opposite.

"Is that any way to speak to one's brother?"

Vane stared down his nose and growled. "You're not my brother but merely the fool who stole my sister away and somehow persuaded her to marry you." He gulped a mouthful of brandy and hissed to calm the heat in his throat.

"Had you the decency to offer your assistance in my search for Estelle, we would not be sitting here." The comment caused Fabian's chest to constrict. A life without Lillian would be a miserable one indeed.

"So let me understand you. It is my fault you kidnapped an

innocent woman. It is my fault your sister ran away and drowned when *The Torrens* sank." Vane paused and closed his eyes briefly before releasing a weary sigh. "Everything is my fault."

A heavy silence hung in the air.

"You should have gone after her." Hell, he should have done something. "Estelle loved you, and you turned your back on her the moment things became difficult."

Vane's penetrating gaze spoke of a cold, merciless anger. "And you think you have the full measure of the situation?"

"What other explanation is there?"

"Perhaps I am the one who was overlooked." Pain flashed across the cool marble planes of Vane's face and vanished with one quick shake of the head. "From my investigation, it seems Estelle met another gentleman in Dover. Together, they sailed away to France to start a new life."

"You're lying." Fabian's pulse pounded in his neck. "Estelle cared for no one but you."

"What the hell have I got to gain by lying? I have nothing to prove to you. I'm going to kill you, anyway."

"And make your sister a widow? I think not." Fabian drained the contents of his glass and refilled it from the decanter. "Besides, regardless of what you may think, my sister is alive." Nothing would convince him otherwise.

Vane sucked in a breath. "Then why waste time kidnapping my sister when you should be out looking for your own?"

A stabbing pain in Fabian's chest forced him to jump up off the bench. Resting his weight on his knuckles, he leant across the table. "I have scoured the streets of London and Paris. I have knocked on doors, harassed strangers in the street. I have followed women, imagining they were her. My eyes convince me I see her ebony hair and kind face, only for my head to berate me for being a blind fool."

"You do not have to tell me what that is like." Vane's hard

tone sliced through the air. "But I will never forgive you for using Lillian."

"For using her? I love her, damn it!" Fabian dropped onto the bench. The love he spoke of filled his heart. "She is the only woman I have ever wanted." It was a love nurtured long ago, a treasure buried beneath bitterness and grief.

Vane stared at him. "You think you're the only man ever to feel that way?" A cynical snort escaped. "It doesn't change the fact that what you did was wrong."

"It was." Fabian could not deny he'd acted foolishly. "Wrong and damnably selfish. But I was not thinking clearly at the time."

"And are you thinking clearly now?"

Fabian considered the question. His love for Lillian lived in his heart and soul, not in his head. It was a pure and genuine emotion. "I would die for her. As long as I live and breathe, no one will dare hurt her again."

Vane frowned. His intense gaze searched Fabian's face. "Lillian has told you about that devil of a rogue Martin?"

"She has."

"Has she told you about our time in Italy?" Vane spoke slowly and with reservation.

Fabian placed his hand at the base of his throat. He could almost feel Lillian's pain. "I know whose likeness she keeps close to her heart."

Vane seemed surprised. He dragged his unblemished hand down his face. "What happened in Italy, it … it broke her."

Evidently, it had affected Vane, too. Anyone could see that a wealth of pain lingered behind his stone facade.

"Then know I intend to do whatever it takes to help her heal."

"I pray you do. Lillian deserves some happiness after everything she's been through." Vane paused and glanced at the door. "Send for her. Let her see you're still alive so that it may ease her fears." He grabbed the poultice and pressed it gently over his knuckles. "That is unless you wish to take this battle of wills to round two."

Fabian chuckled. "I make it a point never to hit a man while he's down."

"Oh, I'm not down. I can hit just as hard with my left hand."

Fabian didn't doubt it. "Perhaps some other time. Besides, I owe you a debt of gratitude."

"Gratitude?" Vane arched a brow. "Why do I sense you're mocking me?"

"It is thanks to Lillian's shooting skills that I stand here today."

Vane shrugged. "Then perhaps I made a mistake in insisting she take lessons."

The ancient door creaked open, and Mackenzie entered. "Is there anything else you need, my lord? If you've no objection, I'd like to venture over to the cottages to check on Mary."

Heavens, the man truly was besotted. "I think we have everything in hand now, thank you, Mackenzie. But can you find Lady Ravenscroft before you go, and ask her to join us?"

Mackenzie hesitated. "Aye, my lord."

Fabian watched him leave. His friend looked troubled. But then unrequited love often made a man sullen and morose. He turned to Vane who was staring at the fan of swords on the wall. "You have the look of a man desperate to demonstrate his parrying skills."

"Not at all." Vane made an odd puffing sound that carried a hint of amusement. "I was admiring the display. Sitting here, one cannot help but feel as though they have journeyed back four hundred years."

"I have always preferred a simplistic life."

"You consider sailing the seas and living on a desolate island simplistic?"

"I consider living anywhere free from the hypocrisy of the *ton* to be an advantage."

Vane gave a nod of approval. "Do you intend to remain here? A community of brigands is hardly an ideal place to raise a family."

"Brigands? They are the most honest, hardworking men I've ever had the good fortune to meet." Well, not always honest. They cheated at cards. Told tales to relieve their boredom. Had shared the odd woman or two. "I'd take my crew over the pompous lords you hold in high esteem."

"Trust me. I care nothing for those weak, insipid sots who live to tour the ballrooms. I have yet to meet a gentleman deserving of my respect." He paused. "That is not entirely true. Lord Farleigh is the only exception."

"Then Lord Farleigh must be a king amongst men."

"He is." Vane gathered his glass and swallowed a mouthful of brandy. "So, have you sent my sister out shooting rabbits for your supper?"

The odd question came as a surprise. "What, you assume because we live a simplistic life Lillian must behave like a peasant?"

"Did you not praise her fine shooting skills?"

"I said she saved my life. Did you happen to see a man-eating rabbit on your journey from the dock?" Fabian couldn't help but chuckle. Nonetheless, the incident with Aubrey was no laughing matter. "During a fight on the heath, Lord Cornell's man pulled a blade and would have used it had Lillian not shot it out of his hand."

Pride flashed in Vane's eyes but faded when a frown marred his brow. "If you have a gripe with Cornell, I would rather you didn't involve my sister."

Fabian recalled Vane's ignorance when it came to Cornell's involvement in the scandal with Lord Martin. Any other time he would have relished breaking the news. But after hearing Lillian's tragic story, it left a bitter taste in his mouth now.

"Cornell is the man who bribed Lord Martin to ruin Lillian." Fabian watched Vane's expression darken. "Cornell's man has been following you for some time, hence the reason he came here. We have him in the dungeon should you wish to question the prisoner."

Like the Devil bursting out of a fiery grave, Vane shot up. "Cornell? You mean to tell me that weasel is the one responsible for ruining my sister's life?" He dragged his hand down his face. "I swear I'll drive my fist through his chest, rip out his blasted heart and eat it for supper."

Under the circumstances, Vane's volatile reaction was to be commended.

"The motive for my recent visit to London was not only to inform you of Lillian's whereabouts but to punish Lord Cornell for the part he played."

Fabian told Vane how he had stripped and taunted the shackled lord.

"Then it seems I am the one who owes you a debt of gratitude."

"I did it for Lillian. To bring an end to her nightmare. To bring her peace."

Vane covered his heart with his hand and inclined his head respectfully. "You should not have let him live."

"If you think that is the end of the matter with Cornell, then you are mistaken." Fabian would not rest until the lord was lying destitute in the gutter. "Sometimes death makes a man a martyr. Humiliation is by far a more just and lasting punishment. Wouldn't you agree?"

Vane sat down. "I don't profess to be a patient man. But the thought of seeing Cornell suffer has appeal. Once I've spoken to

Lillian, and I am assured of her happiness, I should like time alone with the prisoner."

Poor Aubrey. A few minutes with Vane and the thug would confess to all manner of misdemeanours. "As you wish."

Mackenzie returned. He strode towards them but seemed flustered. "Forgive me, my lord. I know you asked me to summon her ladyship, but she's left the castle."

Left the castle? Where the hell had she gone? A frisson of fear coursed through him. But with Aubrey locked in the cell, he had no reason to worry. Had she absconded to avoid Vane's wrath?

"No doubt she's gone for a walk while we settle our dispute," Fabian said to reassure Vane. He turned to Mackenzie. "Inform me the moment she returns."

Mackenzie lingered, his anxiety evident in the way he tugged and played with his beard. "I believe she's gone to the cottages, my lord. I was to accompany her, but errands kept me here."

As a lady trained to manage sprawling country estates, perhaps she thought it her duty to visit the tenants. "She has probably emptied the kitchen of sweet treats and taken a basket to Mary."

"Aye, she intends to visit Mary. After the attack in the bedchamber, no one has seen Mary for two days, and her ladyship is eager to find the culprit."

It took a moment for the words to penetrate. "Someone attacked Mary?"

Mackenzie shook his head. "No, my lord. Someone attacked Lady Ravenscroft. Did she not tell you about the intruder?"

Fabian frowned as a cloud of confusion filled his head.

"Did I not say you lived with a band of brigands?" Vane's hard tone penetrated the silence. "And I heard your men had the utmost respect for you."

"We do." Mackenzie puffed out his chest. "No man here would dare cross the Raven."

"Evidently, you're wrong," Vane countered. "Only a traitorous brute would attack a lady in her home."

"Her ladyship believes a woman attacked her."

Fabian jumped to his feet. He couldn't think clearly. His racing pulse pounded in his ears. "Is there anything else you need to tell me, Mackenzie?"

Mackenzie paused. "Only that in your absence someone has been digging for treasure. Lady Ravenscroft saw two figures on the heathland." His shoulders slumped. "I would have told you sooner, but you've not left the bedchamber since your return."

Vane muttered a curse.

Good Lord! The men had run amok in his absence. "May I borrow a pistol?" Fabian gestured to the duelling pistols on the table. "And your coat."

"I'm coming with you, and only one pistol is loaded. I fired a shot when your man refused me entrance."

"I'm coming, too, my lord." Mackenzie stepped forward. "Anyone who harms the lass will have to deal with me."

"The lass?" Vane raised a reproachful brow. "Are you not taking simplistic living a little far?"

Fabian ignored the comment. "Fetch two swords, Mackenzie, and meet us in the bailey."

They were about to leave when the door burst open, and Ursula rushed in, her clothes sodden and water dripping from her straggly locks. She dropped to her knees before them. "Please, my lord, you must come quickly. Lady Ravenscroft needs your help."

Fabian's blood froze in his veins. He gripped Ursula's arm and brought her to her feet. "Why? Where is she? Is she hurt?"

"I don't know. We went to the cottages to find Mary, but she wasn't there. And so we went down to the dock."

"What do you mean you don't know?"

"We walked the coastline looking for Mary, but someone attacked us from behind." Ursula gasped for breath.

"Attacked you? Was it one of the men?"

She shook her head. "There were two of them, Mary and a man I've never seen before."

"Mary?" Mackenzie spat. "She's lying, my lord. Mary would never hurt her ladyship."

Fabian did not want to suggest his friend was naive, or that love was blind. Women were just as callous as men when it came to deception. "Let us hear the rest of the story before we make any judgements."

"But, my lord—"

"Enough. I must know what these blackguards want." Crimes such as these fell into two categories: a need for money or a desire for vengeance.

Mackenzie covered his hand with his mouth.

"I didn't want to believe it of Mary, either," Ursula implored. "Truly I didn't."

Fabian tried to remain focused. "You mentioned a man. Was it Doyle?"

"Things happened so quickly." Ursula squeezed her eyes shut as if trying to form a mental picture. She shook her head and looked at Fabian. "If it is Doyle, then he is thinner than I remember, and he has a beard. Please. You must believe me. The only reason I stand here is because I'm forced to bring you a message."

Vane remained silent but his intense, unwavering gaze fixed on Ursula.

Fabian inhaled deeply. "What message?"

"You're to travel to Branscombe. You're to bring five hundred sovereigns if you want to see Lady Ravenscroft again."

Fabian cursed and punched the air. So the motive was money. It had to be Doyle. Who else could it be? He wanted to wrap his hands around the bastard's neck and squeeze until his face turned blue.

"Mary is to hold Lady Ravenscroft in a secret location until he agrees to her release."

Mackenzie stepped forward. "May I speak to you alone, my lord?"

"Certainly, but be quick. We cannot afford to linger."

They moved closer to the door, out of earshot.

"My lord, there is no man here more loyal than I." Mackenzie covered his heart with his hand. "Believe me when I tell you, there must be another explanation. Mary despises Doyle and was glad when he left."

Fabian offered a weak smile. "Then we must hope she is acting against her will." He gripped Mackenzie's shoulder. "What choice do I have? It would take hours to search the island. You know that." The sharp stabbing pain in his chest returned. "Damn it all. The man is out for revenge as well as money. If Doyle has taken her to the mainland, we might never find her. I have to follow his instructions to the letter."

Mackenzie's expression darkened. "Then there is no time to waste."

Vane did not ask Fabian how he happened to have five hundred sovereigns to hand. When one lived on an island, a vault was the next best thing to a bank.

The three men, with Ursula in tow, hurried to the dock, commanded a rowboat and headed across the water to Branscombe. They were all soaked to the skin, the torrential downpour hindering their visibility and speed.

"Are you married to a sailor?" Vane asked Ursula as she sat clutching a blanket around her shoulders while they put every effort into reaching the shore.

"No, my lord." Ursula batted her lashes and moistened her

lips. Vane was one of those men who only had to breathe to capture a woman's attention. "I'm a widow, have been these last four years."

"And so you work as a maid?"

"I do."

"I'm surprised one of Ravenscroft's men hasn't made you an offer."

She shrugged her shoulders. "Having once married a man who can drink his weight in ale, I'd prefer to fend for myself."

Fabian knew what Vane was doing. He was testing her, looking for a reason to distrust her word.

"Is it not rather lonely?"

"Why, anyone would think you want to steal his lordship's staff away." For a woman who feared for her mistress, she seemed rather jovial.

"Perhaps I am." Vane flicked a lock of damp hair from his brow. "So, you're not a woman who likes being controlled by men."

"That depends on the man and what you mean by control, my lord."

Mackenzie muttered something incoherent as he heaved the oars.

They rowed in silence, but Fabian could almost hear the cogs working away in Vane's mind.

When they were but ten feet from the shore, Mackenzie climbed out and dragged the boat up onto the shingle beach.

Vane climbed out. "Allow me to assist you." He did not wait for an answer but scooped Ursula up out of the boat, placed her safely on the beach and helped her straighten and smooth her skirts.

"Remind me again what you're required to do," Fabian said as he joined them.

Ursula appeared flustered after receiving Vane's undivided

attention. "I'm to follow the road up to the coaching inn, to the stone that says it's seventeen miles to Exmouth. I'm to leave the money behind the milestone and return to it in an hour for further instructions."

"Very well." Fabian handed Ursula the cloth bag. She struggled to hide a smile, and he knew, with the utmost certainty, she was lying. "We will remain here."

Bag in hand, and with a quick glance back at Vane, Ursula scurried off.

Vane folded his arms across his chest. "How long do you intend to wait before we apprehend her?"

"Give her a few minutes, and then we'll follow."

"I could feel no evidence of a weapon," Vane said. So that was his motive for lifting her from the boat.

"You mean you both know Ursula's lying?" Mackenzie braced his hands on his hips.

"Ever since she batted her lashes at Vane and made flirtatious comments." Any innocent woman used as a go-between would fear for her life.

Vane brushed his hand through his damp hair. "I think we've given her enough time, don't you?"

While Mackenzie waited with the rowboat, Fabian and Vane strode across the shingle beach and down the lane. There was no sign of Ursula at the milestone, no sign of the money hidden behind. A person on the run needed somewhere to hide. A place too dark to search at night, too vast to search by day.

"She's heading for the woods." Fabian pointed to the path further along the lane. They broke into a sprint, splashing through puddles. Water squelched in Fabian's boots. "No doubt she means to wait until we grow tired and leave."

They turned the corner onto the bridle path. There was an hour until sunset, but the canopy of overhanging trees blocked out the light.

A feminine shriek caught their attention, and they spotted Ursula struggling to haul her booted foot out of the mud.

"There you are," Fabian said, reaching her first. "Have you forgotten where the milestone is?"

Impatience got the better of Vane. With a growl of frustration, he grabbed Ursula around the waist, tugged her out of the mud and threw her over his broad shoulder.

"Put me down," she cried as she clutched the money bag so tightly her knuckles were white. "I got lost that's all."

"You can tell us the truth once we're on the boat." Fabian turned and headed back towards the lane. Vane kept a firm grip on Ursula despite sliding about in the mud and almost losing his balance.

"No! You can't take me back to the island." She kicked Vane, leaving mud splatters across his black coat. "I beg you. Keep the money, just let me go. You don't know what he'll do if he knows I betrayed him."

"It's a damn sight less than I'll do to you if he's harmed my sister."

Once back at the rowboat, Vane dropped Ursula onto the wooden bench, snatched the bag of coins from her grasp and held her there while Fabian and Mackenzie pushed the vessel into the water and quickly climbed aboard.

When they were a mile from the shore, Vane released his grip on Ursula and took a turn at the oars. His muscles strained against his coat sleeves as he propelled them effortlessly through the water.

"If you ever have the urge to sail the seas, let me know," Fabian said. "Good men are hard to find."

Vane smirked. "I would rather eat my hat than sleep with a bunch of men for months on end."

"Your rowing skills are second to none." Fabian begrudged paying Vane a compliment.

"I make a point of mastering anything I put my hands to."

"Indeed. At this rate, we'll reach the island in record time."

Ursula whimpered as her frantic gaze shot from the coastline to the blot of land in the distance. "Please. Take me back. I beg you. Don't tell him what I did."

"You're in no position to ask for anything." Fabian stared at her intently. "Tell me the truth. Does Doyle have my wife?"

Ursula fiddled with her fingers and struggled to sit still. "Doyle wants the treasure. Lady Ravenscroft stumbled on his secret hideaway when she sheltered from the storm."

A string of curses escaped Fabian's lips. "I swear I shall kill him this time."

"You may have what's left after I've finished," Vane said.

"What about Mary?" Mackenzie's croaky voice conveyed his unease.

"Doyle has Mary, too. The woman found him digging around the castle at night." Panic infused her tone. She stared at the shrinking coastline. "I've told you what I know, now let me go."

"Not until you take us to Lady Ravenscroft." Fabian would banish Ursula from the island once he'd dealt with Doyle.

Without warning, Ursula came to her feet. The boat rocked and swayed from side to side. Vane and Mackenzie stopped rowing and waited for the vessel to settle.

"I can't go back." Ursula stared at the murky water, her eyes glazed as if lost in her reflection.

And then she jumped.

The splash covered them in spray.

"Good God!" Vane scoured the water, but she failed to surface. "Has she lost her mind?"

"The sea is bitterly cold," Mackenzie said gravely. "A strong swimmer would struggle in these harsh conditions."

A loud slapping and an almighty gasp of breath drew their

attention to Ursula who bobbed and thrashed amid the waves. "Help me!"

"Quickly," Fabian shouted. "Try to remain calm. Try to grab ahold of the oar."

"I can't. It's so cold. It's—" A rolling wave swept over her and then she was gone.

Mackenzie shrugged out of his coat and stood. "Damn foolish woman. She'll be the death of all of us." Without another word, he dived into the icy depths.

"For the love of ..." Vane blurted.

Fabian watched the ripples subside as he waited to glimpse his friend. Mackenzie had been his companion for seven years. To lose him now ... heaven help him, he didn't want to think about it. "Mackenzie!"

After what felt like an eternity, a hand burst from the water and grabbed onto the side of the boat. Mackenzie appeared, one arm wrapped around Ursula's waist. He gasped and heaved as he tried to catch his breath.

"Thank heavens." Fabian's racing heart settled. "For a moment, I feared I might never see you again."

"Aye, my life flashed before my eyes for a second there, too."

Vane dragged Ursula out of the water. It took both men to haul Mackenzie out.

Fabian stared at his friend. "One minute you tell me that the strongest swimmer would struggle to survive, the next you jump in after her."

"That water might be cold to you, but compared to the lochs in the Highlands, it's as warm as a steam bath."

Ursula sat shivering on the bench, her wet hair plastered to her face. "I'm sorry. Please." Her teeth chattered, and she gulped for breath. "I'll do anything to make it right. Anything."

"Good," Fabian said, struggling to feel an ounce of sympathy for the woman. "Because you're going to take us to my wife."

CHAPTER NINETEEN

I n the confines of the dark cave, it was impossible to gauge the time. Hours had passed since Ursula left them to convey the message. God help the woman. Lillian pitied anyone forced to stand in front of Fabian and Vane and deliver such devastating news.

Mary had spoken little. Guilt formed the basis of her reticence. She had apologised numerous times on Doyle's behalf, despite the man showing not the slightest sign of remorse.

"It should not be long now," Lillian said merely to bolster Mary's spirits. "His lordship may find us yet."

Mary looked unconvinced. "Ursula's a sly devil. There's no telling what she's up to. She's been close to Doyle for a couple of years, though having seen them earlier something has changed."

"Your husband is a heartless man." Lillian pictured Doyle's snarling grin as he ripped the locket from her neck. "I don't imagine he's pleasant company when things don't go his way."

"You have the measure of him, although he wasn't like that in the beginning. When his lordship banished him, I hoped never to see him again."

Lillian's heart went out to the woman. When the person who

was meant to fight at your side turned traitor, what hope was there? Mary needed a man like Mackenzie. Strong and dependable.

"Mrs Bell found your cloak pin in the pantry. I left it in my bedchamber and shall return it to you once this is over."

"The pantry? I thought I'd lost it in the cottage." Mary's countenance brightened. Were her hands free, Lillian imagined she would have hugged them to her chest. "It belonged to my grandmother, and her mother before that."

"Having a heart to heart are we?" Doyle approached them. He poked the tip of his boot into the fire and stubbed out the dying flames. "That's enough talking. On your feet. We're leaving."

Though it took effort, Lillian stood. She would spit in Doyle's eye if he dared offer a hand to assist her.

He came to stand in front of Mary, dragged her up by the elbow and pressed his nose against hers. "Don't think you can run from me." He drew a blade from a sheath fastened around his waist and waved it in front of Mary's face. "Stay close else it will be your mistress who pays the price."

Fear should have crippled Lillian, but a sliver of excitement coursed through her when she imagined all the ways Mackenzie would make Doyle pay.

Stuffing his beaten-leather bag with remnants of food, Doyle slung it over his shoulder, waved the knife and gestured for them to walk.

Although Lillian had been in the cave for hours, the storm had not abated. The rain lashed down in torrents, fat droplets bouncing off the rocks nearby. The clouds were black and heavy, weighed down by the enormity of their burden.

"Keep walking." Doyle pushed her in the back as she hovered inside the cave mouth. "Water never hurt no one. This is nothing to the likes of the weather at sea."

With Mary following at her side, Lillian clambered over the

rocks. Having her hands tied behind her back affected her balance, and she slipped numerous times, scraped her knee and stubbed her toe.

The constant roar and rush, rush in her ears made it difficult to hear Doyle's instructions, but they were to head to a cove past the dock. As they battled angry gusts, and waves smashed the shore, Lillian's thoughts turned to Doyle's escape plan. No one could steer a small vessel through these waters. No one could swim any distance in such treacherous conditions.

She turned to look at Doyle. "Surely, you don't mean to navigate the storm in a rowboat?"

The rogue grinned, ignoring the trickles of water rolling off his bald head and down his cheeks. "I've experience when it comes to crossing the sea. Ask his lordship. He's the one who cast me out and left me to the tide."

"From what I hear, you tried to kill the crew."

He said something, but it was lost amid the wind howling a warning. She looked out to sea, to the last slivers of light in the distance, disappearing as darkness chased the sun down beyond the horizon.

Cold, wet, and with her skirts clinging to her legs, she trudged on. The frigate groaned and creaked as they passed the deserted dock.

"The cove is just a little further ahead." Mary pointed into the blackness.

Lillian's heart raced at the prospect of finding Fabian waiting for them. She had faith that whatever Doyle's plan, her husband would save her.

"Stop right here." Doyle's menacing tone reached her ears this time. He grabbed Lillian's bound hands and yanked her back.

Lillian squinted to focus through the heavy downpour. A golden ball of light illuminated the four figures on the beach standing next to a rowboat. A rush of relief made her cry out. "Fabian!"

"Lilly! Has he hurt you?"

Doyle had hurt her in a way he couldn't possibly comprehend. "No." She swallowed down the lump in her throat when she conjured the image of him snatching her locket.

The figures stepped forward until they stood ten feet away. Ursula and Mackenzie accompanied Fabian and Vane. Drenched, the three men looked ready to commit murder. Ursula stood with her hands clasped to her chest. Her lips were blue, and her shoulders shook.

Mackenzie held the lantern aloft, the flame ever flickering. "Tell me you're all right, Mary."

"I—I have had better days."

"Have you brought the money?" Doyle said but offered no excuse or explanation for his villainous crimes.

The coins jingled when Fabian threw a linen bag onto the wet sand. "It's all there. Come and get it."

Vane's penetrating gaze failed to frighten Doyle. In a sudden move, he grabbed Lillian around the waist and brought the blade to rest at the spot where her locket once sat.

Fabian cursed. "Mark my words, you'll pay for this, even if I have to track you to the far ends of the ocean."

"Fetch the bag, Mary, and bring it here." Doyle's foul breath drifted past Lillian's cheek. "Do it now else your mistress will pay the price."

"Then untie my hands."

Doyle hesitated. "Ursula get the bag and come here."

Ursula shook her head. "I—I can't. Keep the money. I'm not coming with you. I'm staying here."

"The hell you are. Get the bag, and get in the damn boat."

Fabian edged a fraction closer. "Ursula has had an epiphany of sorts and finds she must make amends."

After a tense moment of silence, Doyle pushed Lillian in the back and they shuffled forward. With the sharp edge of the blade pressed against her windpipe, Doyle dragged Lillian down to her knees. He picked up the bag and shook it before straightening.

Vane watched intently.

Lillian had seen the same look once before, on the night he caught up with Lord Martin and called him out. Regardless of whether Doyle attempted to ride the giant waves, he was a dead man.

"Well, I'd like to say it's a pleasure doing business with you." Contempt dripped from Doyle's words. "But me and her ladyship here are off on a little journey."

Fabian stepped forward. "You have the money and a boat, now release her."

"I'll not let her go until I'm clear of the shore."

"Och, you've the Devil in you, Jim Doyle, that's for sure."

"But how do you propose—" Fabian stopped abruptly, recognition dawning. "Good God, man! You don't expect her to swim in this."

The wind whined its objection, too. The crashing waves crept ever closer, and she could sense Doyle's urgency to depart.

Vane looked out to sea. He came to stand beside Fabian and spoke quietly in his ear. Fabian shook his head. A frown marred his brow, and he dragged his hand down his face. Vane put a reassuring hand on Fabian's shoulder. Her heart softened at the sight.

"Very well," Fabian eventually said. Gesturing for everyone to step away from the boat, he added, "Leave now while luck is still on your side."

Doyle edged towards the boat. "Ursula? Are you coming? I'll not ask you again."

Shivering and soaked to the skin, Ursula looked up at him. "Why would I come with you when you have ruined my life?"

Doyle shrugged. "So be it." He threw the bag of coins into the rowboat, forced Lillian to climb in and sit on the bench next to him. "We'll need a push."

Fabian stepped forward. He gripped the head of the boat and with a strenuous groan pushed it into the water. "Two hundred yards and then you will release her else I'm coming in after you."

"Push us further out."

With his jaw clenched, Fabian came into the water up to his knees. Waves surged towards the shore almost knocking him off his feet. He stood so close and yet it felt as if he were miles away. Tears threatened to fall. A deep sense of foreboding gripped her. What if this was the last time she saw him? Grief tore through her body.

"Fabian!"

"Be brave," he shouted above the roar of the wind. "I love you."

A rush of heat filled her chest despite her dire circumstances.

Doyle picked up an oar and rowed against the tide.

"I love you," she called back, but her voice lacked the strength needed to rise above the din.

Doyle cursed when the current seemed to take them nearer to the shore. He released the oar, cut the ropes binding Lillian's wrists, waved the knife at her and told her to row.

Fighting the urge to rub the tender skin, she did as he asked.

"One, two, three, heave," Doyle repeated over again.

Lillian stared at the dejected figures on the beach. Mackenzie clutched Mary to his chest. Vane entered the water and stood shoulder to shoulder with Fabian. Ursula stood alone.

"Heave, damn it!" Doyle cried as they hit a huge wave and water flooded the boat.

The spray hindered her vision. She lost her timing. But then it suddenly occurred to her that Doyle had dropped the knife. The further out to sea they went, the harder it would be to make it back. She needed to jump from the boat now before the next wave hit.

Wasting no time, she stood and scrambled over the seat in front.

"Sit down! You'll tip the boat."

Did he think she lacked the courage to swim?

Did he imagine she would let him take her away from everything she held dear?

With one quick glance into the murky depths, Lillian inhaled deeply and then dived into the sea.

The cold hit her like a sharp slap, penetrating her bones in seconds. Water filled her ears. She knew not to panic, knew not to thrash about, knew to wait before trying to move. Erratic breathing only made matters worse. As she surfaced, she tried to keep calm, tried to let her clothes act as a buoyancy as Vane had told her to do. Floating was the key to survival, not swimming.

In calmer waters, her plan may well have worked, but the magnitude and force of the waves sucked her under. She broke the rules. The instinct to swim came upon her, the instinct to fight for her life as the sea swallowed her whole.

But then a strong arm wrapped around her waist and pulled her up to the surface. She gulped air, blinked away the droplets clinging to her lashes. "Fabian."

"Hold on, love. Don't let go."

He swam with her. Perhaps with his experience at sea he knew something she didn't. And then Vane was there, taking his turn, helping them, and somehow they all ended up collapsed on the sand.

Mackenzie and Mary hurried to their side.

"For all the saints," Mackenzie cried, "are you trying to put me in an early grave?"

A weak chuckle escaped Fabian's lips as he gasped for breath. "I said the same thing to her yesterday." He clutched his chest as he sat up. "Good God! Will someone please tell me how we survived that."

The comment focused Lillian's mind, and she sat up and scoured the sea looking for Doyle. "Where's the boat?"

Vane came to his feet. "It overturned." He pointed to the odd-shaped hump bobbing in the water. "The current dragged Doyle under."

Panic almost stole her voice. "M-my locket." She jabbed her finger, her body desperately trying to communicate her meaning. "Doyle has my locket." A whimper became a cry. "No! I can't lose it."

Vane's calm voice penetrated the chaos. "Have no fear. I shall retrieve it."

"No."

Fabian stood. "It is only right I go. Were it not for me, Lillian would not be in this predicament."

"I—I don't want either of you to go. It's not safe."

"If I were a better swimmer, I would go." Ursula stepped up to the water, the flowing tide sweeping up past her ankles and pulling on the hem of her dress. She squinted and stared into the distance. "Do you think he's dead? Tell me he's dead."

Lillian sprung to her feet and rushed forward. "Will the tide bring his body ashore?" She waded in up to her knees, searching for any sign of life. The power of the sea almost knocked her back.

Fabian came to her side and drew her into an embrace. "I'm sorry about the locket. I know it is no consolation, but always remember that no one can steal the love from your heart or the memories from your mind."

Lillian buried her head in his chest and sobbed. They were the tears of a foolish girl, the tears of a woman who'd just come close to losing everything that mattered. She wrapped her arms around his waist and clung on tightly. The sound of his rapid heartbeat soothed her.

"Och, do you think that's wise, man?" Mackenzie cried.

Lillian looked up to see Vane's naked torso diving down far beyond the foamy surf. "Vane!" She broke away from Fabian's grasp, ready to chase after the man who had never forgiven himself for what happened to her. Who would never forgive himself if the only physical thing that reminded her of Charlotte disappeared into the depths of the restless sea.

Fabian caught her by the wrist. "You can't go. Seeing you in the water will only distract him."

"I'll make sure your brother comes back to you, lass." Mackenzie thrust the lantern at Ursula and shrugged out of his coat. He dropped to the wet sand and pulled off his boots. "Had I known I'd be swimming in the sea twice in one night, I'd have come out in just my drawers."

Torn between wanting him to help Vane and wanting him to stay, Lillian said, "Be careful. It's rough out there."

"Och, I swam the waters around the Mealt Falls when I was just a wee laddie. There's no place with a stronger undertow." The Scot jumped to his feet, gathered Mary into his arms and kissed her on the mouth. "Wait here for me, lass. Happen I have things to say upon my return."

Like a Highland warrior of old, Mackenzie charged into the sea and disappeared. They all stood and watched with bated breath. Ursula paced back and forth lifting her lantern high although the wind threatened to blow the flame out. A minute passed before they noticed movement in the water. In the gloom and through the lashing rain it was hard to identify the mass moving towards them.

Without warning, Fabian charged in, grabbed Doyle's body and hauled him to the shore. Mackenzie surged out of the water and sucked in a breath. But where was Vane?

Lillian's heart shot up to her throat.

Tense seconds passed.

Vane emerged. He was on his knees, his chest heaving. Another wave smashed against his shoulders and yet somehow, he scrambled to his feet.

Lillian ran towards them. She reached Mackenzie first, gripped his cold hand and rubbed it affectionately. "Thank you, Mackenzie."

"You're welcome, lass."

She ran into Vane's arms. "I thought I'd lost you."

Vane brushed the stray tendrils from her face. "I failed you once, twice if you count what happened at Vauxhall, but I swore I would never fail you again."

"You have never failed me. You have always been the most loving and loyal brother a lady could want."

His blue lips trembled. "And you are far too forgiving."

Her smile faded when her gaze dropped to his bare chest. Other than in their youth, she had never seen him without a shirt, but the scars shocked her. "What happened to you?" He had one slash mark across his ribs, one across his bicep, two smaller nicks on his chest.

"It doesn't matter. It is nothing for you to concern yourself with."

"Who did this to you?"

"Pay it no mind." He wrapped his hand around her wrist and pulled her to the safety of the beach.

Doyle lay stretched out. Fabian checked the man's pulse and peered into his eyes. He turned him onto his side and thumped his back but to no avail. Fabian stood and shook his head. "He's dead. One of us will need to head to the mainland to alert the authorities."

Ursula's gasp spoke of relief.

"I'll go," Mackenzie said. "But first, I'll take the body to the warehouse on the dock."

"Wait. Check his pocket." Lillian's pulse raced at the prospect of seeing the precious necklace again.

Fabian bent over the lifeless figure and rummaged in his trouser pocket. He withdrew the chain and delved deeper to find her treasure. Clutching the items in his hand, he strode over to her and placed them carefully in her palm.

With trembling fingers she tried to open the clasp, but her hands were too cold.

"Allow me." Fabian prised it open. He stared at the image before handing it to her, and then he cupped her cheek and smiled. "She's as beautiful as her mother."

It took Lillian a moment to rouse the courage to look. Water had seeped inside to wet the edges, but the image remained intact. She closed it quickly and clutched it to her chest.

"We should all head back to the castle," Fabian said. "We need a hot meal, a roaring fire and dry clothes. We can alert the authorities tomorrow."

Ursula hung her head. "What about me?"

"You will come with us for now until I decide what to do with you."

Vane threw his wet shirt over his head and shoved his feet into his boots. "I'll help Mackenzie move the body and meet you back at the castle."

Fabian inclined his head. "As you wish."

"I'll go with Mackenzie, my lady," Mary said, "unless you have need of me tonight."

Lillian smiled. "No, after a hot bath, I shall be fit for nothing but my bed."

Fabian stood beside her and took hold of her hand. "Come. We shall reconvene in the morning and discuss how best to proceed then."

Mackenzie hauled Doyle's body over his shoulder and, with Ursula following sheepishly behind, Vane and Mary accompanied him to the dock.

Once alone, Fabian took Lillian in his arms. "I cannot think of another time in my life when I've been so afraid. If I'd lost you —" His voice cracked.

Despite the rain, for how could they possibly be any wetter, she twined her arms around his neck and kissed him. It was a kiss unlike any they had shared before. It spoke of a soul-deep connection. An unbreakable bond. It spoke of a desperate need to make every second count.

Lillian pulled away. "When I speak, can you hear me above this incessant roar?"

"Yes, why?" He wiped the rain from her cheeks.

"Because I want to tell you that I love you. Because I want you to know it is a love that took root long ago, one that has grown deeper over time."

He bent his head and touched his forehead to hers.

"I have loved you from the moment you stuck your tongue out at me when you were eight. Perhaps even before that. There has never been anyone for me but you. You are the matching half that makes me whole."

"That's rather poetic."

"I cannot take the credit. They are Aristophanes' words, but the sentiment is mine."

"It is a sentiment I share."

They held hands and strolled back to the castle.

"And what of the treasure?" she said. Was it all nothing more than a drunken tale? "Do you believe the Spanish hid gold here and never returned to claim it?"

Fabian shrugged. "I don't know what to believe. But why chase a dream when the only treasure I need is at my side? One day we will tell our children the story. It can be their legacy, their treasure to find."

By the time they reached the gates, the black clouds had dissipated to reveal an inky sky bright with stars.

"And what would your philosophers say if they could comment on the night's events?" she said as they entered their bedchamber.

"Were they alive today, I imagine they would draw on the words of Vergil."

"What, that all bad fortune is conquered by endurance?"

"No." Fabian wrapped his arms around her waist. He pressed his lips to her cheek, trailed hot kisses down her neck. "That love conquers all."

CHAPTER TWENTY

The he midday sun shone, and the waves broke calmly on the shore as Fabian and Lillian stood with Mackenzie on the landing pier.

"Och, had a twenty-foot wave not swept me off my feet, I'd struggle to believe there'd been a storm."

No matter how pleasant the day, Fabian would never forget the moment he came close to losing Lillian. "Violent storms bring devastation. Thankfully, only those deserving felt the full force of nature's wrath." Fabian captured Lillian's hand merely to reassure himself all was well.

"I doubt I'll travel in a rowboat again without taking a spare pair of breeches." Mackenzie patted the leather satchel draped over his shoulder and winked.

"You have the letter?"

"Aye."

"Lord Trevane will accompany you when you visit the magistrate. I suggest you both make a statement. Trevane has business in London and will not want to delay." The need to discover Estelle's fate burned in Fabian's chest. She had plunged into the sea with *The Torrens* and survived. But what then? Vane's warning that most people had an identical counterpart failed to rouse the faintest flicker of doubt. "A speedy inquest is advisable, and so offer to ferry the coroner and the jury to the island posthaste."

"Aye, I'll let Lord Trevane do the talking. I doubt anyone would refuse that man anything. Besides, the sooner they declare Doyle officially dead, the sooner I can marry Mary."

Lillian squeezed Fabian's hand. "I take it she accepted your proposal."

"Aye." A faint blush touched Mackenzie's cheeks. "I think I impressed her when I charged into the sea like a Viking warrior."

Lillian came up on her toes, placed her hand on his shoulder and pressed a kiss to his cheek. The highly familiar gesture made the man's face flame. "I wish you both well. After everything that's happened, you deserve to be happy."

"Yes," Fabian said. "Perhaps when you have a wife to occupy your time I might take my bath in peace."

"Having seen you rescue her ladyship from the stormy sea, there's no fear of you drowning in the tub." Mackenzie laughed. "Right, I'd best climb aboard. Trevane is on his way, and the lord likes things done at the click of his fingers."

"I'm afraid my brother lacks patience and tolerance, is often hot-tempered, but beneath it all he has a good heart."

Mackenzie's gaze softened. "I know enough of men to know what ails him, lass."

Lillian sighed. "Well, let's hope in finding Estelle, he finds himself."

The thud of booted footsteps on the wooden pier caught their attention. Vane strode towards them, his black clothes impeccable after Heather had dried, cleaned and pressed them.

Mackenzie said a quick goodbye, bowed and climbed down the wooden ladder to the rowboat.

As Vane approached, he glanced at the vessel and grinned.

"After witnessing my skill with an oar, I expected to be the one rowing us to the shore."

"After exerting yourself last night, I wasn't sure you be up to the task." Fabian suppressed a chuckle. "Freddie and Skinny will ferry you across to the mainland. I assume you stabled your horse in Branscombe."

"Yes, but now I wish I'd brought my carriage." Vane yawned. "I hardly slept a wink last night. Whose idea was it to put me in the room next to the Scot? The man snores like a bear."

Fabian pursed his lips. Needing time alone with his wife, he'd wanted Vane far from their bedchamber.

"Did you gain any information from Aubrey? Mackenzie said he gave you access to the dungeon this morning."

Devilish was the best way to describe Vane's grin. "The man is nothing more than a scout though I hope you gave him a clean pair of trousers before sending him on his way."

An hour earlier, Isaac had taken Ursula and Aubrey to Sidmouth. Fabian wanted rid of Aubrey before the coroner came, and, quite frankly, Ursula could do whatever she pleased as long as she never set foot on the island again.

"One look at Aubrey's scarred face and I doubt anyone would dare comment."

"He has an extra bruise or two since last you saw him," Vane said.

"Only one or two?"

"I used my left hand. I must give my right hand time to heal should I encounter trouble when scouring the rookeries."

Lord, surely that was the last place Estelle would go. "Thank you for agreeing to search for Estelle." Fabian had no choice but to swallow his pride.

Vane shrugged. "Thank Lillian. She's the one who is rather persuasive."

Fabian reached into his coat pocket and removed the

miniature of Estelle. "Here, you may borrow this." He offered Vane the picture. "It has been some time since you last saw Estelle. This might help to refresh your memory."

Vane swallowed numerous times. His eyes glazed as he stared at Fabian's hand. With some hesitance, which was highly uncharacteristic, he took hold of the oval frame.

"Thank you. It may prove helpful." He did not look at Estelle's image but simply placed the miniature in his pocket.

"Are you certain you don't need my help?" There wasn't a street or establishment in London Fabian had not searched.

Vane shook his head. "I prefer to work alone."

"I have men posted in Paris and Calais. Another man in Dover." Fabian retrieved a note from his pocket and handed it to Vane. "Should you wish to contact them, here are their names and directions."

"Once I've spoken to the coroner, I shall head to Dover and speak to your man. I see little point going to France until I've exhausted all other possibilities." Vane cleared his throat. "You understand that the chance of finding her is slim at best."

"Of finding her alive, you mean." Fabian could tell from Vane's expression that he believed Estelle had perished on *The Torrens*. "She is out there. I know it. Don't ask me how or why."

Vane said nothing and simply inclined his head.

"Will you remain at the house in Berkeley Square?" Lillian said.

"For the time being, though I shall send word should my circumstances change."

"Please." Fabian was not used to begging. "Should you see Estelle, inform me immediately."

Vane gave a curt nod. "I should go. There is much to do."

Lillian rushed forward and wrapped her arms around him. "While I know you must try to find Estelle, part of me wants you to stay." She sniffed. "We have been through so much these last two years."

Vane cradled her cheeks in his hands and wiped a tear away with his thumb. "You belong here, anyone can see that, though I advise you to refrain from swimming when the sea is rough, and the tide is high."

Lillian gave a weak chuckle. "But I want you to be happy as I am."

"We all have a path to follow. Mine deviates from yours, but that changes nothing between us." He glanced briefly at Fabian. "Ravenscroft will care for you in my absence. You will have a family, a house filled with love. That is all I have ever wanted for you."

Fabian watched them embrace, wondering if the day would ever come where he might say the same to his sister.

"Now, if I don't get in that boat, Mackenzie will grow tired of waiting and is liable to swim to the shore."

Lillian stepped back and sucked in a breath. "Then go now. We shall visit soon."

Vane turned to Fabian. "Keep her safe. I hold you personally responsible for her welfare."

"Of course." Fabian inclined his head. He drew Lillian close as they stood and watched the rowboat move away from the pier.

"Do you think he will find her, Fabian?" Lillian wrapped her arms around his waist. "Do you think he will ever be happy?"

He wanted to believe both were possible. "The truth is I don't know. But if marrying you has taught me anything, it's that the mind is a powerful thing. Belief is everything." Fabian only hoped he had enough to make up for Vane's misgivings.

She looked up at him. "Do you say that because you had faith that we would weather the storm?"

"I say that because I called you and you came."

She drew her brows together in confusion.

"Come," he said. "Let me show you what I mean."

Together, they ambled along the clifftop path, stopping only to watch the rowboat disappear into the distance. Once at the castle, he asked Lillian to wait for him while he rushed to the bedchamber and picked up a book. Then he took her hand and drew her up to the roof of the keep.

Despite the mild weather, they were so high the wind ruffled his hair. He flicked to the relevant page and handed her the book.

"You see," he said. "I knew long ago we belonged together."

Lillian scanned the relevant passage, her eyes growing wide.

"Read the last line aloud." He wanted to hear the words fall from her lips.

"It says … *each of us is a matching half of a human whole… each of us is always seeking the half that matches him.*"

"And what did I write?" He remembered the moment clearly, a cold, miserable night at sea when he sat alone in his cabin.

"You wrote my name." She brought the book to her chest and hugged it. "You wrote Lillian Sandford."

"I have stood up here many times and thought of you."

She shook her head. "Why didn't you say so the night you first brought me here?"

"Because I am a fool, a man once blinded by bitterness. Because for a moment I lost faith and feared rejection." He reached up into her hair and pulled out the pins. The wind took the rich, ebony locks and blew them free. "I hope I have gone some way to make amends. I hope I have satisfied your quest for freedom."

"It is not freedom I seek anymore. I want to share everything with you. I want you to stake your claim on me, body and soul."

"Then know that I, too, am yours to own." He smiled and gestured to the vast ocean. "Look out and tell me what you see."

She stared at him, an intense look of love and longing that

warmed his blood. "How can I look at anything else when the magnificence of the man before me commands my attention?"

How different things were now to the night she arrived.

"Sailors stare at the horizon longing to be somewhere else. Those with sorrow in their hearts stare at the sky longing for an epiphany."

"And what do those in love do?"

He drew her closer, took the book from her hand and threw it to the floor. "Allow me to show you."

Their lips met in a kiss that spoke of a deep abiding love. A love that could heal broken hearts. A love that promised hope for the future.

Thank you!

Thank you for reading *The Scandalous Lady Sandford.*

If you enjoyed this book please consider leaving a brief review at the online bookseller of your choice.

Read the next book in the series
The Daring Miss Darcy

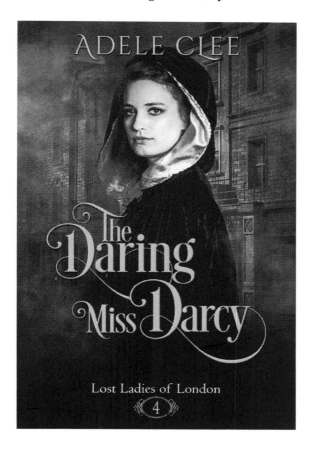

Books by Adele Clee

To Save a Sinner

A Curse of the Heart

What Every Lord Wants

The Secret To Your Surrender

A Simple Case of Seduction

Anything for Love Series

What You Desire

What You Propose

What You Deserve

What You Promised

The Brotherhood Series

Lost to the Night

Slave to the Night

Abandoned to the Night

Lured to the Night

Lost Ladies of London

The Mysterious Miss Flint

The Deceptive Lady Darby

The Scandalous Lady Sandford

The Daring Miss Darcy

Printed in Great Britain
by Amazon